‐

P'

S

v

F

T

s

"Now Who's Seducing Who?"

Michael pushed Bree back against the wall, and his lips found hers. He kissed her hard and long. Glorious heat rushed through her veins as she kissed him back.

He lifted his head. Dazed, her heart racing, her eyes met the wildness in his gaze. He was the father of her unborn baby. In spite of all the walls she'd tried to erect against him, she still felt connected to him.

What she really wanted was for him to love their child and maybe someday love her, too. And when he kissed her like this, some idiotic part of her believed that could happen, that he might change someday, that he might see her as she was and be capable of respecting her...of loving her.

Her Pregnancy Secret

ANN MAJOR

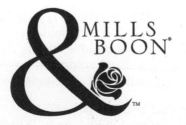

First published in Great Britain 2014
by Mills & Boon, an imprint of Harlequin (UK) Limited,
Large Print edition 2014
Eton House, 18-24 Paradise Road,
Richmond, Surrey, TW9 1SR

© 2014 Ann Major

ISBN: 978-0-263-24432-8

Harlequin (UK) Limited's policy is to use papers that are natural, renewable and recyclable products and made from wood grown in sustainable forests. The logging and manufacturing processes conform to the legal environmental regulations of the country of origin.

Printed and bound in Great Britain
by CPI Antony Rowe, Chippenham, Wiltshire

ANN MAJOR

lives in Texas with her husband of many years and is the mother of three grown children. She has a master's degree from Texas A&M at Kingsville, Texas, and is a former English teacher. She is a founding board member of the Romance Writers of America and a frequent speaker at writers' groups.

Ann loves to write—she considers her ability to do so a gift. Her hobbies include hiking in the mountains, sailing, ocean kayaking, travelling and playing the piano. But most of all, she enjoys her family. Visit her website at www.annmajor.com.

To Ted
I love you more

One

Michael North awakened with a violent start in the middle of the night.

His first thought was for the safety of the exquisite woman curled trustingly against him. She was warm and soft, beguilingly beautiful in the moonlight with her dark golden hair spilling across his pillow. He wanted to touch that hair and kiss her lips again, wanted it so much he had to clench his hands.

Ironically, he'd enjoyed his evening with her more than he'd enjoyed being with anyone in a very long time.

Maybe that was why his gut twisted as he experienced an uncustomary pang of conscience.

After all, he'd seduced her for very deliberate, self-serving reasons.

Careful not to disturb her, he sat up and brushed a lock of thick black hair out of his eyes. Everything he'd done tonight—the seductive dinner at her failing bistro, the lovemaking in his penthouse, all the shared laughter and smiles—had been a lie.

He'd set her up so he could protect his naive younger brother.

But at some point Michael had forgotten about Will. His dinner date with Bree had begun with champagne served in sparkling flutes at Chez Z, the intimate French bistro she'd inherited from her famous brother, Johnny Z. She loved to cook and to eat, and Michael had loved watching her indulge.

She'd blushed when she'd drunk champagne. She'd sighed when she'd licked chocolate off her fingertips, and his. The wet, warm tip of her tongue against his flesh had almost been as good as having sex with her. *Almost.*

He'd loved the sound of her laughter, the glow of her cheeks when she teased him, the flash of intelligence in her slanting eyes when she'd made him feel clever and her wildness in bed. When had he had such a good time with anybody?

Surprisingly, Bree had given him more pleasure and tenderness and amusement during their evening than he'd ever imagined possible.

Because, first, she wasn't his usual type. He went for cool, sophisticated glamour, for sleek, slim blondes who made heads turn and other men envy him. Bree was lush and earthy and wanton. She loved color and baubles and cheap scarves and probably didn't bother to carry a comb in her purse.

And second, Bree Oliver, for all her seeming innocence and charms, was a gold digger. She'd targeted his foolish brother, thinking Will was the chump she needed to keep Chez Z from going into bankruptcy.

For Will's sake, Michael had to finish her off. No matter how much he'd enjoyed being with her or how fabulous she'd been in bed, she deserved it.

If only Michael had been as smart five years ago when he'd fallen for Anya Parris. But, no, like a fool, when Anya had lied about being pregnant, he'd married her. He'd suffered through a hellish marriage that had included infidelity, scandal and a very public divorce.

Never again would Michael forget the cynical truth about the North wealth. It attracted women who pretended a genuine interest in him when all they wanted was the use of his penthouse, his ranch, his helicopters, his private jets, his invitations to the right clubs, the best restaurants and the A-list parties. Unlike his brother, Michael wasn't above enjoying the women his money lured, but only for brief intervals.

Never again would he believe any woman wanted more from him than his luxurious lifestyle. Never again would he make the mistake of forming a serious attachment. Unfortunately Will, who'd had a more indulged childhood than Michael, was too trusting for his own good. It was up to Michael to save Will from Bree.

Soft summer moonlight turned the high ceilings of his loft and his large bed to shades of silver and gray. Bree's body felt warm; treacherously so as she nestled closer against him. Her cheap silver bangles and necklaces on the bedside table glittered. Her colorful, filmy clothes and scarves lay in tangles on the floor beside her sandals where he'd stripped her while she'd swayed to music, laughing.

The cozy heat of her satin-soft body lured him. He wanted to stay beside her, to see the shy warmth of her sweetly crooked smile and the flirtatious glow that lit her amber eyes every time he kissed her.

No, he had to finish her off—now—even if her sweet strawberry scent filled his nostrils and made him weak with the craving to bury his lips in her thick, satiny hair, to kiss her throat, to taste her mouth and other parts of her sexy, feminine anatomy just one more time.

Intoxicated by her soft, sensual allure, he lingered in the bed beside her, torturing himself as he savored her warmth and remembered all the ways they'd made love.

She'd been so silky and tight the first time, like a velvet glove. When he'd pushed eagerly inside, holding her against the wall, she'd cried out. But when he'd stopped out of concern for her, she'd pressed her palms into the small of his spine and pleaded with him to stay—to stay forever if that was possible. Slowly her small body had accommodated itself to him. Driving into her, the pleasure of each stroke had been so total in its visceral thrill that fierce pleasure unlike any he had ever known had saturated every cell in his body.

She'd been a damn good actress, playing at virginal innocence, enticing him, then surrendering like a wanton. She'd nearly undone him. She'd almost made him believe that he alone, not his fortune, was special to her.

"Who knew?" she'd whispered with him sheathed inside her. "I like it. No, I love it." Then she'd stroked his cheek lovingly, her eyes shining with wonder. "I'm glad it's you. I never thought it would be half so nice. I always wanted to date someone as handsome and smart as you. I...I just never thought anybody like you...would look at a girl like me."

It had been nice for him, too, being with her. More than nice.

Special.

His world could be so cold, and she seemed so sweet. For one forbidden moment, when she'd kissed him as if she'd wanted to consume him, he'd lost himself in the searing hot, torrid welcome of her body. He'd almost forgotten to protect himself.

Every time he'd made love to her, even with a condom, the sex had gotten better. And each time afterward when she'd clung to him, she'd seemed sweeter. Whatever this thing was between them, it had shaken him to the core. Hell, just thinking about her and what she'd done to him made him hard again, even as he lay beside her icily plotting his next step.

"Will said you were cold and uptight," she'd whispered.

He hadn't liked her comparing him to Will, but with every kiss and unassuming glance her power over him had increased. A connection to her built deep inside him and morphed into something that felt more than physical.

What had been going on?

Her mysterious white-hot appeal had fueled a compulsion that no other woman had ever aroused in him. She'd made him ravenous. Together their writhing bodies had burned and soared. His out-of-control excitement had felt addictive, tempting him to forget everything he knew about women like her. She'd provided some deeply needed comfort he hadn't known he'd craved until he'd experienced it in her arms. He had never known a real home, or felt at home with anyone, not even with the Norths, who'd given him their name and had claimed him as family. Not until tonight... with her.

She was dangerous. He had to rid himself of her quickly.

If he stalled for even one more night, she might have him totally in her power. He might even sink his own money into her bistro.

If he invested enough, would she favor him over Will?

Hell, he had the money. A part of him wanted her to prefer him to all others.

He swore. Such thoughts could derail him from his purpose. Just as he was about to throw off the covers and escape her so he could get his head straight, she whimpered. Clutching at his arms, she seemed to expect him to protect her from some mysterious terror.

"Michael..."

His heart throbbed. Oh, God.

Her voice was feminine, helpless. When her featherlight fingertips brushed his skin, he burned, aching for her all over again. No way could he resist her plea.

How old was she? Twenty-five? Ten years younger than he was? Or even younger? Whatever her age, with her thick, dark gold hair tumbling about her face and bare shoulders, her wild beauty dazzled him. She had a classic brow, a long, thin nose, high cheekbones, an incandescent complexion and full, voluptuous lips.

Not that she had the money or sense of style to dress properly. Her baggy, overlarge clothes had concealed and distracted more than they'd enhanced her beauty. But naked—with her tiny waist, curvy hips, soft breasts and those pert nipples exposed—she was perfect.

More than anything he wanted to roll her over, take her in his arms, hold her and pet her hair, and whisper that everything was all right. But nothing was all right. Not when he knew what she was—and what he had to do—and yet still felt so powerfully attracted to her.

Careful not to disturb her, he arose. He had to get a grip. But the minute he broke their physical connection, she sensed it and seemed to miss his presence as much as he missed hers.

"Michael," she purred in a sexy, sleep-blurred tone. "Darling, come back to bed."

"I'm not your darling," he growled, hating that on some level he wanted to be.

"Michael, I… Have I done something…?" At his harsh tone, her voice grew shy and uncertain before it died in the silvery darkness.

The powerful need to comfort her from the hurt he was determined to inflict wrapped around him.

Hell. He had to finish this—or he would go crazy.

"I'm not your darling," he repeated ruthlessly. "Tonight, everything, all of it—it was all lies."

"Lies?"

"I seduced you to protect Will. From you. When you came on to me while I was with him at the fund-raiser, I knew what you were and saw how you intended to use him. You made my job easy when you made a play for me, too."

"What are you saying?"

"I'm saying I sought you out tonight and slept with you so I could use it as leverage to make you stop seeing my brother. Tonight was all about Will."

"Will?" She sounded confused. "Wait a minute. You think Will and I...that we're a couple? That we're dating? You...you don't like me?"

"How could I like you, knowing what you are?"

Having been poor himself, he knew all about wanting more, about using people to get what he wanted. He'd worked damned hard. Still, he'd done a few things he wasn't proud of to get where he was.

"You were after him, and then after me, because you needed our money for your failing restaurant."

"No," she whispered.

"Do you deny Will is one of your investors?"

"No." But her beautiful mouth trembled just a little, and her eyes were now glistening with unshed tears. "You...deceived me? You didn't really want me?"

He shook his head.

"Why? How could you do that? I would never use Will...or anybody. Will's a friend, and yes, he's an investor. He's been an investor right from the beginning. But I'm not after his money! I'm not!"

"Then why did you hit on me so blatantly the night we met at the fund-raiser when you were with Will?"

"Maybe I flirted. But only because I thought you liked me...." She sucked in a breath. "Will is just a friend. He was a friend of Johnny's first, and an investor in Chez Z when my brother first opened it. That's how Will and I became friends."

"Friends? That's all you were?"

The night of the fund-raiser she'd worn a silver backless gown and a transparent shawl that had left very little of her sensuous shape to his imagination.

Her family history hadn't helped his opinion of her. Six months ago, Johnny Z, her celebrity-chef brother, had been found dead in bed with a prominent plastic surgeon's wife, another of the bistro's investors. Everyone presumed the surgeon had shot Johnny, but the husband, who'd hired lawyers, wasn't talking to the police, and his wife had vanished. Thus, the investigation had stalled. Still, the scandal, coupled with Z's absence in the kitchen, had been devastating to Chez Z's bottom line.

"Will asked me to go with him to the fundraiser, so he could introduce me to some people who might be interested in investing. When he introduced me to you, I thought you might be one of those people."

Her eyes were so brilliant with innocence and outrage he almost believed her. Then he remembered Anya and how gullible he'd been. He'd wanted to believe her. Capable as he might be in the business world, apparently he was an easy mark when it came to women he wanted in his bed.

"Bottle the performance! If you think I'm as big a fool as my little brother, you're wrong. I want you to dress and leave. If you stay away from Will, I won't tell him I slept with you tonight. If you don't leave him alone, I'll tell him about us."

"Tell him for all I care. Better—maybe I'll tell him myself. He needs to know how far you'll go to control his life. Maybe he'll resent you even more than he already does."

Her reaction caught him off guard. He'd expected her to care more, to bargain, and what she'd said about Will hurt.

"He can't afford to resent me," Michael bluffed. "I write his allowance checks."

"So everything's just about money and control to you? And you think I'm like you—"

"I know you are! So, leave my brother alone, and I won't make him think the worst of you by telling him about us. You bet on the wrong horse this time. Pick another. Someone who isn't naive. Someone more like you and me."

"Tell him. I'm not like you, and you can't blackmail me, either."

"You are like me. Greed isn't the only thing we have in common," he replied coldly. "If Will didn't desire you, I'd be willing to set you up as my mistress. I'd keep you and your bistro afloat for as long you excited me."

"*Do you ever listen?* For the last time, your brother and I are just friends. That's why he won't care if you slept with me. He was just an investor in the bistro. He already has someone in his life."

"Really—who?"

Michael knew she was lying when she faltered and said, "Maybe you should ask him."

If only Will did have someone, then Michael could have Bree for himself. He could afford her a helluva lot more easily than Will, couldn't he?

Suddenly Michael reconsidered the situation. Where was the harm in keeping her, if she wasn't serious about Will? As long as he understood what she was and was willing to be generous to her?

"Okay, then, *if* Will doesn't want you because he has someone else, there's nothing to stop me from having you. Here's a new deal for you. If you cut Will loose as an investor and become my mistress, I'll keep your bistro afloat for as long as you please me in bed."

"What?" She stared at him as if she was having a hard time comprehending him.

"You heard me. Be my mistress, and your money problems will go away for as long as you keep me happy. Like you did tonight."

"I can't believe this. First you sleep with me to destroy an imagined relationship with your brother. And now you want to buy me for yourself? I'm sorry I ever met you."

"I'm sure you'll feel differently after you shop for the right apartment in the neighborhood of your choice and we settle on your generous allowance."

"Now you wait a minute!"

"You want to save the bistro, don't you? We enjoy each other, so why not?"

She pushed herself up from the bed. "You can't just buy people!"

"You'd be surprised what money buys."

"Well, I'm not for sale."

"I doubt that. I just haven't made you the right offer. Tell me what you want, and we'll negotiate."

"I can't believe I ever thought for one second that you were a decent human being." Her expression twisted in utter misery. "And I did. I really did. I can't believe I've been such a fool…again." She sighed. "This just proves what I told you earlier—I don't have very good instincts about men. I think you're the worst of them all…and I have to tell you, that's pretty low."

Her rejection stunned him. Too late Michael saw that he should have flattered her, that he should have seduced her into the deal as he had seduced her into his bed. Obviously she was like all the criminals in prison who proclaimed their innocence; she really didn't see that she had done anything wrong. That's where they were different. At least he knew when he'd crossed the line and was willing to accept the inevitable consequences.

"I'll call my chauffeur," he said coldly, hiding his disappointment. "He'll be at the front door downstairs in five minutes to escort you out of the building. He'll drive you anywhere you wish to go. After tonight I don't ever want to see you with my brother again. Do you understand?"

"You can't order me around…or your brother, who is an adult, and who is, whether you like it or not, one of my key investors. I fully intend to see him as often as I like! He has every right to invest *his* money where he chooses."

"You're very wrong."

Michael turned his back and strode out of the room because the sight of her shimmering, pain-filled eyes, her quivering lips and her bare breasts were more than he could bear. Damn it, in spite of her rejection, in spite of what she was and how she was using Will, he still wanted her.

Only when he heard her rushing down his spiral staircase to the lower floor—she never used an elevator unless she had to because she was afraid of them—only when he heard his front door slam downstairs, did Michael return to his bedroom.

For a long moment he stood in the dark and stared out at the city that sparkled beneath a full moon and a starless sky. It was a beautiful night, he supposed, a night made for romance, if one believed in such things. He wondered if his failure to do so was due to the many flaws in his soul.

Growing bored with the view he left the window and turned on every light. Never had the vast marble bedroom in his penthouse apartment blazed with such cold and terrible brightness.

Only when he saw the bright splashes of red staining his sheet did he realize that maybe he'd been wrong about at least one thing.

Had she been a virgin? His heart, which usually felt so solid behind its frozen walls, began to beat with vicious, guilty pain. Surely no virgin would have shown such a wild, uninhibited response. And yet…

When he remembered her little cry when he'd first entered her, and her sweetness, and the admiration in her eyes when he'd discussed some of his projects with her, he recoiled. What if she had been an innocent? What if he, who'd been raised so roughly, had failed to see goodness because it had been such a rarity in his life?

"If I could succeed at even one thing, I'd feel so proud of myself," she had confided. "And look at you—you turned the family investment firm around right after the last global financial meltdown. Now you're opening banks and hotels in China and power plants in Malaysia. You conquer worlds—and accept such feats as your due. Your family must be so proud of you." Her shining eyes had warmed him through.

If he'd been wrong about her virginity, had he been wrong about other things? Had she truly admired his accomplishments? Had she liked him, at least a little? Had he wounded her? And what was she really to Will?

No.

Damn it. He was sure of her ulterior motives. With her famous brother dead, his image trashed and their once popular bistro on the Upper West Side in trouble, she'd been after Will for his money. Then she had zeroed in on Michael at the fund-raiser when she'd seen a better mark. The only reason she'd turned down Michael's second offer was because he'd wounded her pride.

As he yanked the sheets off his bed, he remembered her radiant complexion and the wonder in her eyes and his own intense pleasure. Sheathed to the hilt, he'd felt all male and powerful and yet happy in a bone-melting way he'd never known before.

If she was what he believed, why had she turned him down? Why?

Michael tried and failed to push his gnawing doubts aside. Damn it, he had to know why. But he couldn't face her tonight.

They both deserved a few hours to recover from his brutal offer and her rejection. Tomorrow morning would be soon enough to confront her again.

But by morning she was gone.

After he bribed the doorman to let him in to her empty apartment, he stomped about flinging her cupboards open while he dialed her cell phone, which went to voice mail. For more than an hour he searched for some clue as to where she'd gone and found none. His texts were ignored. When he went to Chez Z, her steely-eyed French mother, Bijou, had been in a meeting with the waitstaff.

"She said she had to go somewhere," her mother said coolly, when he'd insisted upon interrupting her. "She said it was an emergency. She looked upset. I didn't pry. Now, I wish I'd asked more questions. Are you the problem? Is she in trouble because of you?"

"No."

"Well! She is no good with men. In fact, that's an understatement. She's *pathetic*. She took after me, you see. Her father did everything he could to ruin my life. If you aren't going to treat her right, stay away from her, yes?"

What could he say to that? Despite the circumstances, he envied Bree for having such a mother. He hadn't been so lucky.

When Michael went to his brother's to warn him about Bree, Will refused to let Michael into his apartment.

"She already told me what you accused her of," Will said, standing with the door half-closed to keep Michael in the hall. "I don't know where she is, and frankly, I wouldn't tell you if I did. You've overstepped the line."

"She said you were seeing another woman? Are you?"

Will, who usually had an easy nature, scowled.

"Right now, maybe you can guess why I don't choose to discuss my personal life with you."

Then he shut the door in Michael's face.

Michael felt guilty and uneasy. What was Will hiding? Not only had Bree rejected him, she'd turned his brother against him. Will wouldn't even confirm he was dating someone else, so did that mean he was still interested in Bree? If Will was involved with another woman, what the hell had Michael accomplished by bedding Bree other than becoming obsessed with her himself?

The odds were he was right about her character. Maybe she was gone, but what good was that if Will felt more protective of her than ever? Instead of turning his brother against her, all he'd done was make his brother angry with him.

Despite everything, Michael burned for her. No matter how hard he tried to bury himself in his work during the weeks that followed, no matter where he traveled or how many glamorous women he publicly dated in the attempt to prove to himself and to her how little she mattered, he couldn't forget her.

Even when he left on what proved to be a month-long business trip to Shanghai to solve a

crisis at one of his hotels, memories of her sweetness and outraged innocence lingered, haunting
him.

The perfection of their night together drove him
mad—especially after he learned that the same
day he'd left New York, she'd returned to her bistro and had lunched with Will.

Had she deliberately remained hidden until he
was gone? Was she that afraid of him?

What was her game? How could he stop her
and save Will?

Two

Eight weeks later

*W*ill *has to be okay. He has to be.*

As his heart beat in panic, Michael slammed through the heavy steel emergency-room doors with his dripping briefcase. When Pedro, his assistant who'd notified him about the accident, wasn't at the entrance, Michael had rushed inside and hurried down a crowded hall that was a blur of nondescript floor tiles and pale green walls, beds, patients and visitors.

Michael had been trying to call Bree from his limo on the drive through thick rain from JFK airport into the city. When all he could get was her voice mail, he'd decided to stop by Chez Z on the way to his office to confront her again. He'd just pulled up at the curb outside the bistro when Pedro had called him to tell him Will had been in an accident.

"Where's Will North?" Michael demanded of the nurses in dark scrubs at the nurses' station. "I'm his brother. I got a call a while ago that he was in an accident and that he'd been brought here by EMTs."

"North?" Nurses looked up from their papers and stilled. When they didn't answer him, maybe because they had to choose their words carefully, he sensed the gravity of his brother's condition.

Oh, God. It was bad.

"Where is he?" Michael demanded in a hoarse voice he didn't recognize as his own. "What happened?"

Ask a tough question....

An older nurse with a kindly face gave him the bare facts.

A head-on collision in the heavy rain. Tony Ferrar, who was apparently his brother's friend and the driver, died at the scene. The driver of the SUV that struck them, a twenty-four-year-old woman who'd possibly been drunk or texting, had flown across the median of the interstate and collided head-on with Will's Mercedes. She'd died at the scene. Will had removed his seat belt and thrown himself in front of his wife. As a result he'd suffered back injuries, head injuries and multiple fractures. He needed immediate surgery.

The nurse's words buzzed in Michael's head.

"Wife?"

Was that what Will had wanted to tell him over lunch today? Had he married his secret girlfriend?

On some level Michael's numbed brain faced the harsh reality of his brother's injuries. On another, he refused to accept that his younger brother could be so seriously injured.

Not Will. Michael had called him from Shanghai last night. When Michael had asked him about Bree, Will had refused to discuss her.

"I have some big news. I'll give you an update over lunch tomorrow," was all he'd said.

"Can I see my brother…before his surgery?" Michael demanded of the nurse.

"Of course. But don't say much or you'll tire him."

Only when he saw Will's gray face washed of

all color, and Will's body shrunken and as still as death did the gravity of Will's injuries finally hit Michael.

"Will. Can you hear me? It's me. Michael," he said gently.

Tubes hissed and gurgled. His brother, whose bruised face was swathed in bloodstained bandages, stirred faintly. His mouth quivered, and he seemed to struggle to focus on Michael's face.

"Don't talk," Michael commanded.

"Have to… No time… You know, they're wrong about your life passing before your eyes." Will's voice was so thready Michael had to lean close to his brother's lips to hear it. "It's the future you'll never have…that matters."

"Don't waste your strength trying to talk. You're young. You're going to be okay. I swear it."

"Not even you can fix this. But you can do one thing for me…."

"Anything."

"Take care of Bree."

"What?"

"Bree… She's…my wife," Will gasped.

"Bree? You married Bree?"

"She's pregnant. No time to explain. We didn't want to tell you like this. Just promise me…that you'll take care of her and…the baby."

"The baby?"

"She's pregnant and hurt. I don't know how badly. We were in the backseat. Tony was driving. Tony's dead…. Tried…to save her…for you."

"For me…"

"You care about her."

Sweat broke out on Michael's forehead. His hands opened and closed in fists as fury and concern for her and grief for his brother tore at him.

One thing was very clear. She'd lied about her relationship to Will. They had been involved. After she'd slept with Michael, she'd gone back to Will as easy as you please, gotten herself pregnant by him so he'd marry her. They'd kept it all a secret from Michael until he'd gotten back from Shanghai.

Will had been so dazzled by Bree he'd removed his own seat belt to protect her.

Then Michael remembered that Will would receive a million dollars from the North trust when he married, as well as a sizable increase in his allowance. He would receive even more once the child was born.

Had Will informed Bree about all those benefits? Probably.

Her treachery didn't matter right now. Only Will mattered.

His brother's glazed eyes read Michael like a book. "I know you don't think you like her. And I knew you wouldn't approve of our marriage, but she's been through a rough time. She's a wonderful girl. Not a gold digger like you think."

Michael swore silently. His brother was so hopelessly naive.

"What you did to her…was all my fault."

"Whatever I did, I did it for you," Michael said.

"Understood. So, promise me…you'll take care of her. If you'll do this one thing for me, we'll be square."

No way could Michael promise that.

"Promise me," Will insisted.

The room felt stale and airless. His brother looked so pale—Michael couldn't say no to him. He yanked at his collar and tore at his tie that was damp from the rain. He wanted to run out of the room, to get outside, to breathe fresh air.

Through gritted teeth he said, "I promise I'll take care of your wife." Carefully Michael took his brother's limp hand and pressed it lightly. "I'll even shake on it."

"And her restaurant. Help her save it."

Michael nodded.

Satisfied, Will's heavy eyelids drooped shut.

A few seconds later an older male nurse in blue scrubs rushed up to the gurney and flipped through Will's chart. Without a word, he bent over his patient.

Michael stood in the doorway and watched the man wheel his brother away, watched until they vanished down the long hall. The sounds of people rushing past him died. All he could hear was his own heart. Would he ever see his brother alive again?

Suddenly he felt very cold, and very much alone, as alone as he'd been as a kid. Since he couldn't stand forever in an empty hall staring at waxed floor tiles and feeling sorry for himself, he turned and headed back to the nurse's station where he found Pedro, who took Michael to Bree.

Two women, probably family, hovered over

Bree. She lay on a narrow bed that had been cur-
tained off from the other beds in the large room.

Michael held out his hand. "I'm Michael North,
Will's brother. Her brother-in-law."

The older woman took his hand. "I'm Bijou, her
mother. Wait! I never forget a face. You're that
handsome rich guy that came to the restaurant
looking for her, yes? I thought maybe you gave
her some trouble, yes?"

Heat washed through him. "Yes."

"I'm Marcie," the pretty blonde beside Bijou
said. "I wait tables for Bree and Bijou. Bree's
just the sweetest person in the whole world. So
is Will. I can't believe that two such super people..."

"Marcie! You need to be strong, *oui!*" Bijou
turned to Michael. "We'll give you a minute with
her," she said. "But only a minute."

When they left, Michael moved closer to Bree's
bed. Her thick lashes were still against her blood-
less cheeks, so she didn't see him at first. Dark
circles ringed her eyes. More than a dozen bruises
and livid cuts covered her arms and cheeks. At
the sight of her injuries, he choked on a breath.

She looked so slim and fragile in her hospital

gown, he felt a stab of fear. She was carrying his brother's child, and Michael had sworn he'd take care of her.

Despite the money she must have been after when she'd married Will, Michael's resentment toward her faded. If Will died, her child would be Michael's last link to his brother.

"Bree? Can you hear me? It's Michael. When I got in from Shanghai I heard about the accident. I came at once."

"Michael…" Her lashes fluttered weakly, and for an instant her face lit up with pleasure…and with some other more luminous emotion that thrilled him. Her eyes had shone like that when he'd first entered her.

In the next second she must have remembered what he'd done because her gaze went flat and cold. "Where's Bijou? What are you doing here? I want my mother back."

"Your mother's right outside. Will asked me to check on you, so I'm here," Michael said softly.

"Will asked you…" She let out a harsh sob and turned her face to the wall. "I don't believe you! He's as fed up with you as I am! Go away!"

Michael felt conscience-stricken and confused, which wasn't like him.

"I don't need you here," she said to the wall, her tone so low he could barely hear her. "Will knows that, so you're lying if you say he sent you."

"He did. He was facing surgery, and I think he was afraid."

She sucked in a breath. "Oh, God… I'm being so selfish. Tony's dead and maybe Will won't… and he's in there scared and alone…and thinking of me. He's so good."

"Yes, he is." Michael's voice was hard and condemning.

When she jerked her head around to stare at him again, he noted how the soft blue fabric of her hospital gown molded against her breasts. "They told me how badly Will was hurt. They didn't want to. But I made them. If he dies, it will be all my fault. He took off his seat belt… right before that SUV shot across the median and rammed us. Will saw it coming and threw himself in front of me…to protect me and the baby. Poor Tony never had a chance."

"Who's Tony?"

An odd, almost sorrowful expression passed

swiftly over her bruised face. Clutching her sheet, she looked away. "Will's best friend. He was driving."

"Funny. I've never met him."

She chewed her bottom lip. "I imagine you were too wrapped up in money matters to really involve yourself in your brother's personal life—except when it came to me—because you saw me as a financial threat."

Her words hurt more than they should have. "Will said you and he were expecting a baby."

Her face went even whiter, if that were possible.

"H-he had no right to talk to you about the baby. He swore to me he wouldn't."

"He asked me to take care of you…and the baby…in case…"

She shuddered. "It just gets worse, doesn't it? You and me—stuck together…maybe without Will?"

"It's probably just a precaution. I promised him I would. If…if the worst happens. I intend to keep my word."

"Really? Your word?" She tipped her head back and frowned, studying him. "As if that means something." She took a deep, stabilizing breath. "Just go away."

"I intend to honor my promise—whether or not you want me to," he said.

"You deliberately deceived me, to get me to do things I find truly humiliating now. How could I have been so foolish?"

Sensual, erotic things he'd dreamed of her doing to him again.

"I thought I'd found the one person—never mind!" she snapped. "You made it very clear how you really felt about me at a moment when I was most tender and open and vulnerable to you. I don't know how all those other women feel, the ones you date for a night or two, but let me be very clear. You are the last person I would ever want in my life, even casually. I don't care if you're Will's brother and my baby's…uncle, or that you feel a duty to keep your promise. I do not want to see you. I do not want my child to know you. Do you understand?"

Her words cut Michael deeply. Curiously, he felt guilt, as well. Why should he feel that when he'd been trying to protect his tenderhearted brother who had proven time and again he was too trusting when it came to people who were after his money?

Not that Michael showed his pain at her words by even the flicker of his dark eyelashes. Having grown up poor, in a rough Houston neighborhood near the ship channel, he'd learned to put on a tough mask whenever he felt the slightest weakness. His mother had barely eked out a living as a masseuse before Jacob North had married her and adopted him.

Until Jacob, his mother had gone from man to man, taking whatever they offered to survive. Michael had worked on the docks so he wouldn't be dependent on such handouts. He'd hated having nothing and being treated like nothing and feeling ashamed of how they'd lived. He'd learned early on that when you didn't have it, money was everything.

Will, on the other hand, had grown up a rich man's adored only son. Will had loved everybody, especially his older adopted brother, whom he'd accepted right from the first. Maybe Will was the only person who'd ever loved Michael. He'd promised Jacob, to whom he owed everything, that he would look out for Will. Those feelings of profound responsibility carried over to Will's unborn child, even if that child's mother was someone he could never trust.

"If Will dies, Will's child—your child—will be a North heir. Then there's the promise I made to my brother. Whether or not you want me in your life, I intend to take a very active interest in that little person from now on."

"So this is about money and control? My child is nothing more to you than the possible heir to the North fortune."

Why should he let her know what Will's child meant to him when she would only use such knowledge against him?

"A fortune does carry a huge responsibility."

"I'll bet you're used to getting your way."

She was right about that.

Her eyes darkened. "Well, you won't. Not with me. Never again."

"We'll see," he said. Then he let it drop. He fully intended to win this battle, but he wouldn't bully the pregnant wife of his injured brother.

"I want you to go," she said.

"Too bad."

When he sank down into the chair beside her

bed, she glared at him. At his thin smile, she shut her eyes and twisted her face away. As he stared at her stiff back, he knew she couldn't force him out of her thoughts any more than he could force her out of his. Just being in the same room with her, even when she was injured, disturbed him.

An hour later, she was still rigid and seething when Will's grim, hollow-eyed surgeon found them.

"Mr. North? Mrs. North?"

When she opened her eyes and met Michael's, she blushed.

"I'm Will North's wife," she said. "Michael North is my brother-in-law."

"I see. Sorry about the confusion."

Michael had only to look into the surgeon's shadowed eyes to know the worst. Will was gone. Slowly Michael stood and shook the man's hand, listening, asking the appropriate questions, thanking him even as ice closed around his heart.

Bree let out a hoarse sob midway through the surgeon's detailed explanation.

"Your brother lost a lot of blood at the scene...."

Michael's vision blurred. He felt himself near some fatal edge. Maybe to steel his own nerves, he concentrated on Bree, whose face had gone as white as her sheets. Leaning over her hospital bed, he took her trembling hand. At his touch, she stiffened. Then, to his surprise, her fingers tightened around his, and she tugged him closer. Grabbing fistfuls of his jacket, she threw her wet face against his broad shoulder and burrowed into it. Clinging to him, she wept soundlessly.

His suit would be a mess tomorrow, but he needed to hold her, needed it more than he had ever imagined needing anything. Despite his own hideous sorrow and the profound gulf that separated them, he was glad Bree was here, glad not to be completely alone with his grief.

"Bree," he murmured. Careful not to hurt her, his arms closed around her. "It's going to be okay."

"You don't know, so how can you say that?"

"Time has a way—" He broke off, unable to repeat the usual trite phrases people offered one another for comfort.

Strangely, holding her seemed to be enough. Never had he felt more powerfully connected to another human being as her tears rained down his cheek.

After a long time she said, "Tell my mother and Marcie…about Will. Please…" Her voice was choked. "I just can't."

"Anything," he murmured as he let her go. "I'll do anything you want."

"Really? Excuse me if I find it hard to believe that the man with no heart is now willing to do anything for me."

"You're pregnant with Will's child, and he's gone. Everything's different between us now."

"Yes. Will's child," she repeated softly.

"There's nothing I wouldn't do for Will's baby, and, therefore, for you."

Three

The pain meds must have made her daft. Why else would she have agreed to spend the night—no, seven nights—at Will's loft with Michael?

Because your Victorian brownstone has stairs—three tall flights of them—and no elevator, remember?

The fact that her building had no elevator had never been a problem before. Okay, so she didn't like elevators or any small, boxy room. With her history, who would?

When she'd been a kid, an older cousin had locked her in a closet and left her there while he'd gone out to play. She'd been hysterical by the time her mother, who'd been busy in the kitchen downstairs, had found her. Every time the doors of an elevator closed Bree remembered Jeremy's gloating smile right before he'd shut the door and turned out the light.

Bree chewed a nail as Michael jammed the key into the door of Will's loft apartment in the Village. Maybe if she deliberately goaded Michael, he'd decide looking after her wasn't worth it.

"I can't believe, that as frequently as you saw your brother, you've never been inside his place before now," she said.

Michael's mouth tightened. "What do you know about it?"

She smiled. "Oh—did I hit a nerve?"

"He used to have me to his place on the Upper East Side all the time," Michael snapped, "but for some reason he didn't want me dropping by anymore when he moved here. Usually we met at my penthouse or somewhere in the city. I did stop by a couple of times, but he was either just going out or his roommate was home and they were busy. I didn't understand why he needed a roommate when he could have easily afforded to live alone. When I asked him about it, he said the guy was a good friend who needed a place to stay."

"R-right," she said uneasily, deciding to back up Will's lie. "He…he was still living here when we married."

"Must have been crowded, you two being new-lyweds and all."

She didn't like his tone but refused to comment.

When Michael finished unlocking the door, he caught her elbow to usher her inside.

Startled by the fire in even that brief touch, Bree jumped back. How could she feel anything for a man who'd used her and had lied to her? He was the last person she wanted helping her. But he *was* Will's brother.

"This really isn't necessary," she said, hoping she didn't sound as nervous as she felt. "You don't want to be stuck with me any more than I want you here. Why don't you make it easy on us both and just leave?"

"I'm staying," he said in a tone that was raw and intense. "You can fight about it. Or you can make the best of it. Your choice."

The carved lines of his face looked powerful and strong—implacable. She was much too weak, exhausted and woozy from the pain meds to fight him. When he nudged her inside, she let him.

"Whoa!" Michael said, obviously taken aback by the dramatic design of the apartment and its furnishings. "This is truly amazing, totally different than his other place. I didn't know Will had something like this in him."

There's a lot you didn't know about him.

Strangely, the thought made her feel sorry for Michael.

Tony, who was a top designer and world-famous in certain circles, had put the apartment together. Not Will. The airy rooms with their skylights and soaring ceilings, and dramatic art collection and colorful, minimalistic furnishings screamed Tony.

Not Will, and not her. It wouldn't be long before Michael picked up on the fact that she hadn't really lived here.

Maybe there was a piece of paper from city hall that said she and Will were married, but there was very little of her here. A chipped coffee mug or two, a pair of her jeans and panties and a favorite sweater with a cat on it in the single drawer Will had emptied for her.

She'd slept on their couch for a couple of weeks wondering how she'd ever forget Michael and get clear of the mess she'd made of her life because of him. The only two things she'd been sure about were that she wanted her baby and she wanted to get Z's bistro back on its financial feet. Will had promised to help in every way he could, both personally and financially.

"I really think I'll be fine on my own here."

"Hey, we've been over that. You heard what the doctor said," Michael murmured in the same gentle, mesmerizing tone he'd used to seduce her. "You're pregnant. You have a nasty bump on the head. Your blood pressure is a little low, and you shouldn't be alone for the next week."

He *almost* sounded concerned.

Reminding herself that he didn't care about her, she also reminded herself that she was okay with that. She refused to care about anybody as cold and unfeeling as him. She stepped farther inside, only to feel truly trapped when he slammed the door, stripped off his expensive jacket and flung it toward the sofa.

"I don't want you here. You are the last person

I want to be with tonight when I feel so utterly miserable."

"Understood. Ditto."

"Underline ditto," she cried.

"But here we are—together." Grimly, he bolted the various locks from the inside. "It might be dangerous for your baby, my niece or nephew, if I don't stay. Like you said, your mother has cats, and you're allergic to them."

Why was he acting as though he cared?

"From what the papers have said lately, I'd think you'd surely have some gorgeous supermodel waiting in your bed to welcome you home from China," she muttered, dragging her gaze from his wide shoulders.

After the fund-raiser when she'd been so dazzled by him, she'd researched him online. She'd been dismayed to learn about all the glamorous women he dated. After her one night with him, he'd gone right back to dating those women. How could she have thought he was interested in her that night? The eagerness she'd felt for him and the things she'd done in his bed still mortified her.

His jet brows winged upward in cynical surprise. "Jealous?"

Despite her grief and exhaustion, hot indignation that he'd hit a nerve flared inside her. "Only you, who are so arrogant and sure of yourself, would take it like that."

"Yeah, only me—the number one ogre in your sweet, innocent life." His grin was savagely ironic. "You didn't answer my question, sweetheart. Are you jealous?"

"Don't be insane! It's just that I couldn't help noticing an item or two about you and several models in the gossip columns. Did you go out with them to destroy them, too?"

When a muscle jerked in his jawline, she almost wondered if she'd hurt him. Then she remembered he didn't have a heart.

After an ominous pause, he said, "There's no supermodel…if you must know. Hell, there's nobody waiting, which is pretty normal. So, tell me about you and Will. I was shocked when he told me you were married, especially after you'd told me you weren't interested in him that way. How did it happen? And when?"

She turned away to hide her eyes, lest she give

something away. "He asked me. I said yes. Unlike you, he's a really nice guy."

"Which made him perfect prey for a woman like you."

"You're wrong. About him and me." She stopped. There was no way she could defend herself without getting into deeper trouble.

"Forget it," she said. "I don't care what you think."

But she did.

Frowning, Michael paced the length of Will's dazzling white room with its grand piano and splashes of paintings and sculptures. He stopped abruptly to look at the photographs of Will and Tony on Tony's piano.

Panic surged through her when he lifted one.

"Who's the big guy in leather?"

She moved toward the shiny black piano. Not that she had to see the picture up close to know that it was Tony in his trademark black biker attire with rings in his ears. In the photograph, he and Will were toasting Johnny and her at a party at Chez Z. It had been only a few months ago, to celebrate the restaurant's success. Will had been ecstatic to be part of a successful venture and to share his happiness with Tony.

Tears misted her eyes. How could so much change so fast? How could they both be gone?

"It's Tony," she said

"The driver? He was Will's best friend who died at the scene? He was Will's roommate, too?"

"And our best man," she said.

And so much more.

Michael slowly set the picture back on the piano beside the others of Tony and Will with different friends. "Tell me again why you married Will."

She backed away. "Do we have to talk about this?"

"You asked me about *my* love life." A dangerous edge had crept into his soft voice. "Did you want him, my brother, as much as you wanted me?"

It made her sick to remember how much she'd wanted Michael; sick to think that even now he wasn't entirely unattractive to her. She wanted to believe he wasn't the man she knew he was, wanted to believe he cared, at least a little. But he'd told her in no uncertain terms how he felt about her, so she steeled herself.

"I married him, didn't I?"

"Why?"

Because of what you did to me. Because your wonderful, caring brother wanted to help me and take care of me, which was something he knew you'd never do. Because I didn't know what else to do.

He seemed to sense her vulnerability. Her heart skittered as his large, tanned hand closed over hers, making escape impossible. His dark eyes flashed with alarming passion as he drew her to him.

She averted her gaze from his handsome face. He'd been so cruel, and she'd fought so hard to forget him. Why couldn't she? He'd only had to walk into her hospital room this afternoon to make her remember how he'd dazzled her.

Then he'd accused her of being a gold digger and worse.

"I've thought about you," he muttered. "Thought about that night, about everything we did and said, even though all I wanted was to forget you. Even now—when I know you were lying about your relationship with Will all along, you still get under my skin."

Ditto.

Feeling on the verge of a meltdown, she tried to wrench free. It was clear that he'd hated his involvement with her, that he wanted nothing to do with her. And it still hurt—more than it should have, even now when she knew how cold and cruel he was.

When his burning eyes stared into hers, she began to shake because she was terrified he would see her pain and understand how gullible she still was.

He held on to her and drew her closer. "How the hell could you marry my brother?"

Her pulse thrummed. As always when she was in his arms, he aroused forbidden needs.

She had to remember he'd deliberately used her, not caring how he hurt her. He still despised her. She couldn't trust anything he said or did.

Michael certainly did not deserve the truth.

"Why did you marry him?" he asked again.

"It's complicated."

"I'm good at complicated, so tell me. Or better yet, show me," he whispered.

"I don't know what you mean."

"Don't you?"

Suddenly his hands were in her hair, stroking the dark silken gold that fell against her nape. His fingertips followed the sensuous curve of her neck before he cupped her chin and lifted her slender face to his, his touch as gentle and seductive as it had been that night.

Frantically, because it would be so easy to lose herself to the emotions that blazed in his eyes, she fought to resist him.

If only he had a real heart. If only she could truly depend on him and didn't have to be afraid of how she felt. But she knew, and even so, he aroused her.

Her skin burned and her knees went weak. He had only to touch her to make her yearn for his tenderness. Had there been a night since she'd seen him last that she hadn't ached to have him hold her like this and make her feel loved again? To look at her as he was looking at her now, with eyes that devoured her, adored her?

The craving for all the things only he could make her feel became too much to resist. Without thinking, she arched her back and opened her lips, inviting his mouth to claim hers. His tongue entered her. In an instant, the rightness of his searing kiss, and her hunger, were a thousand times stronger than what she'd experienced before.

She had to fight him. She knew what he was about. But the room was spinning and she was clinging, melting, falling. As he pulled her closer, every feminine cell pulsed with the desire to surrender to him in the hope he felt something deeper than he could admit.

All that mattered was that she'd longed for him, and he'd returned. She felt him, erect with a fierce masculine need he couldn't hide as he pressed against her. No matter how he'd denied his feelings, there was a raw, elemental truth in his kisses. In that moment she believed he was as helpless as she to fight the explosive chemistry between them.

Again and again he kissed her, leaving her shaken from the bittersweet joy of being with him again. His tongue dipped deeply inside her mouth and sent a tremor through her. When his grip tightened around her waist, she realized he was trembling even more than she was.

Time seemed to slow as he made love to her with his mouth and tongue, as his hands moved down her curves. She'd missed him, though she'd denied it.

She couldn't deny it now as his hands slid downward to cup her bottom and bring her closer to the powerful, masculine heat of his arousal.

Throwing caution aside, her hands traced over his hard body before sliding inside his waistband. In her desperation she ripped his shirt out of his slacks. But when she caressed his hard abs, he shuddered, let out a savage cry and then tore his lips from hers.

Cursing her softly, he took a step backward, even as he retained a grip on her arm to steady her when she began to sway.

"What's wrong?" she whispered, aching for more.

"You answered my question," he said, his cold, flat voice reducing the tenderness and warmth that burned inside her to ashes. "You still want me—which means you married Will for cold, calculating reasons. You are every bit as low as I thought. I'll never forgive you for using my brother like that. You didn't care how you were going to hurt him, did you? Not as long as you got what you wanted."

"What?" In shock, her wild eyes met his icy ones.

Who was using who? How could Michael kiss

her like that and then shut her out again just when she felt so passionately aroused and open to him? Just when she believed there might be feelings beneath his passion. Had he really kissed her like that only to prove a point?

She swallowed and fought to find some control within herself, but she was too close to the edge, too vulnerable. She had been through too much today. She wanted Michael, and he despised her.

"I don't want you. My resistance must be low because they gave me painkillers. I—I didn't know what I was doing."

"Well, you can believe that if it makes you feel better," he began with a calm disdain that chilled her to the marrow. "But you want me, all right."

Because I'm a human being, and I thought you cared.

"So, do you need help undressing or running a bath?"

"What?" His curt, dismissive change of subject hurt.

Surely she would lose all self-respect if he stripped her and touched her and made her even more aware of him as a man while he regarded her with such cool contempt.

Never again would she let him arouse her deepest feelings and play her for a fool. *Never again.*

"I can take care of myself," she snapped, furious. She was weak and injured tonight and that had made her highly susceptible. He'd taken advantage of her.

"Then I suggest you get started," he said.

"I don't want to bathe with you here."

"Then pretend I'm not here."

"Impossible."

"The only reason I'm looking after you is because I made a promise to my brother. Trust me, I'll leave you alone. I didn't kiss you because I wanted to. I kissed you to find out if you wanted my brother, the poor bastard. You didn't. So, go in the bedroom, shut the door and get ready for bed."

How could she stay here with him? How could she pretend he wasn't here while she undressed, when awareness of him still buzzed in her blood despite his icy disdain?

"While I'm waiting for my turn to shower, I'll see what there is to eat and make some business calls."

"Right—the all-important CEO who's always

so busy looking after the North fortune he doesn't have time to be human."

"Damn you, I've got other things to do besides babysit you. I've got work," he growled. "Lots of it." Turning his back on her, he pulled out his phone and sank down on the couch.

Infuriating man.

Whoever answered on the other end must have begun by offering his or her condolences immediately because Michael lowered his voice and hunched over the phone, his expression haggard as he talked about Will. So, he wasn't totally unfeeling. He just didn't care for her.

Her heart constricted as she heard him going over some checklist about funeral arrangements, and Bree imagined he'd forgotten her. Surrendering to his will, partly because she couldn't bear to listen as he finalized the details of Will's memorial service, she padded softly toward Will and Tony's bedroom.

As she entered it, Michael cupped the receiver. "Don't lock the door," he ordered. "If you faint, I'll need to get in. If I can't open the door, I'll break it down. Do we understand each other?"

Exhaustion and frayed nerves and what was left

her desire had her so close to the edge she felt like screaming. Or weeping hysterically. "You're such a brute! I don't want you here. And I don't have to do what you say. I don't! I can't stand you!"

"We've already had this discussion. The doctor released you on the condition you'd remain under my care until your checkup next week because you were spotting. You agreed."

As if he cares about the baby, she thought dismally.

"Next week!" she moaned aloud. "I was in so much pain, I was out of my mind to agree to a week with you."

"Bottom line—you agreed," he said. "So, you'll damn well do what I say, or I'll make you!"

She shut the door. Then, thinking about the way he'd kissed her and rejected her—as if she was nothing—she opened the door and then slammed it so hard its frame shook. Not that the childish action gave her any satisfaction.

Her gaze ran over the guys' bright, modern bedroom. Being in Will and Tony's private space brought the loss she felt for them to the surface again. They'd been so sweet to her. Feeling confused, grief-stricken and concerned about her unborn baby, she went into their bathroom where she stared at her white, bruised face in the huge, carved mirror they'd told her they'd bought on a recent trip to Oaxaca.

Cuts and purple bruises covered her gray skin. Blood stiffened several locks of her hair. How could she have imagined Michael desired her?

He didn't want her. He never had, and he certainly didn't care about her. No, he disliked her. He'd seduced her to drive a wedge between her and Will. Tonight he'd kissed her and used his expertise at lovemaking merely to prove that he had her where he wanted her. His only interest in her had always been using her to protect the North fortune. For that same reason, he was interested in the baby. The baby was his heir.

If only she hadn't agreed to Will's plan. Then Michael wouldn't be here, and she wouldn't have kissed him again and relearned how powerfully she still felt about him. Nor would she have had to endure realizing how much he despised her.

Choking back a sob, she began to strip.

Michael couldn't stop thinking about Bree alone in Will's bedroom.

Had she and his brother been happy in that bed

together? Even though a part of Michael hoped she'd made his brother happy, another more self-ish part resented any connubial bliss, however short-lived, she might have shared with Will. Because the idea of her in any other man's bed, even his brother's, felt like sacrilege.

She was Michael's. He wanted her. Kissing her again had taught him how much.

Why was he always attracted to users like her? God, what a mess.

How many endless, bleak hours had passed since she'd slammed the door? With his arms pillowed under his head, he felt restless on this couch from hell that was too short for him. He stared up at the bar of moonlight shifting on the ceiling.

Michael had promised his brother he'd look after Bree. He'd come here intending to honor his promise. What had he done instead? He'd mauled her just because he'd had to know if she still desired him.

She did. Her molten response had almost brought him to his knees.

He had no right to touch her. No matter what else she was, she was his brother's widow. She'd been injured in a car wreck that had claimed three lives. She was pregnant, and her condition was precarious. For her protection and the baby's, he had to keep his hands off her.

His eyes grew heavy, but just as he was about to shut them, she screamed. His heart racing with fear, Michael bolted to his feet and raced across the shadowy apartment.

He pushed the door open. "Bree?"

She'd kicked her sheets and blankets aside and was shivering. When she neither cried out nor answered him, he realized she was having a nightmare. His fault, no doubt. She'd been through a lot, and he hadn't made things easier for her.

His anger forgotten, he rushed to her. The masculine, long-sleeved dress shirt she'd chosen to wear had ridden up to her knees. When he saw the paleness of her bruised face and the dark shadows under her eyes, his concern and the self-loathing for his callous treatment of her grew.

Instead of awakening her, he pulled the covers over her gently. When she continued to tremble, he went to the living room and grabbed his jacket. He draped it over her shoulders. Then, unable to leave her, he sank down onto the bed beside her. After a long moment he began to stroke her hair.

Asleep, she looked young and innocent and completely incapable of deceit. He remembered the blood on his sheets that first night and how virginal she'd seemed when he'd made love to her. He'd never been with anyone who'd seemed so young and fresh and eager for him. Although he'd told himself she'd been a clever actress, he'd been enchanted. He'd almost forgotten that he'd ever considered her opportunistic and out to deceive his naive brother.

When she cried out again and then, drawn by his warmth, cuddled against him, he hardly dared to breathe for fear he'd startle her.

Then her hand slid across his thigh and a flame went through him. In an instant he was as hard as granite.

With her soft body lying against him, it was much too easy to forget why he should dislike her, much too easy to remember the heat of her response.

"Michael," she whispered. "Michael."

"I'm here," he said, worried that he'd awakened her somehow.

"I'm…baby…I'm having a baby. Wanted to tell you…but didn't know how."

"It's okay." He looked down at her.

Her lashes were shut. He relaxed when he realized she was only talking in her sleep.

"I know about the baby," he said. "It's all right."

"I wanted you to be happy about it."

"I am happy about it."

He was happy his brother had left something of himself behind. At the same time, illogically, he wished she'd never been involved with Will.

Unable to resist the temptation to touch her and reassure her, he placed his hand on her shoulder. Then very gently he brushed his lips to her forehead.

"Don't be afraid," he whispered. "I won't let anybody hurt you…or your baby. I swear."

In her sleep, she smiled. "I know. You just pretend…to be mean and awful and greedy."

The wistful tenderness in her voice touched his heart. As before, she smelled of strawberries, making him remember how slick and tight she'd been, how she'd cried out at his first stroke—just as a virgin would have—but then had refused to let him stop. She'd felt so perfect. She'd been so sweet.

The memories had him burning up. His every muscle felt tight. The blood on his sheets had been real. He'd been her first. She hadn't been lying about that as he'd tried to make himself believe. No matter what she was, that had to mean something.

He wanted to pull her closer, to hold her, to ask her why she'd never slept with anyone before him. But more than that, damn it, he wanted to make love to her again.

What was he thinking? Why did he care so deeply for this woman who'd only wanted his brother's money?

He had to get up and separate himself from her before he lost all control and kissed her and woke her…and risked jeopardizing her health and the baby's.

Gritting his teeth against the pain of leaving her, he eased himself to the other side of the big bed. Then he got up and went to the window where he stood for a long time, staring down at the glittering rooftops of the Village. Not that he really saw the sparkling lights or the buildings in the moonlight.

He couldn't let himself feel so much for this woman.

When his breathing eased, he walked over to Will's easy chair beside the bed and sat down. He intended to stay only a minute or two, but Bree's sweet nearness eased the savage demons that rode him.

No matter what she was, no way could he leave her alone to deal with her nightmares.

Before he knew it he was fast asleep.

An alarm buzzed in her ear. When she moaned and rolled over onto soft, downy pillows, her throbbing head felt foggy. Every bone in her body, indeed every muscle she had, screamed in pain. Where had this headache from hell come from?

She let out a smothered cry and sat up. What was wrong with her? Why did everything hurt?

"You okay?" growled a deep, protective voice from above her.

In confusion she blinked up at the tall, broad-shouldered man towering over her. "Michael?"

What was he doing in her bedroom?

Confused, she scanned the bright paintings on the walls. No, she was in Will and Tony's bedroom.

As Michael's black eyes continued their blazing appraisal, she blushed at the intimacy of awakening in yet another bedroom with him.

How long had he been watching her? What was she doing here with him?

In the next instant his tense, brooding expression had her flashing back to him sitting beside her in the hospital. She remembered the SUV careening across the median straight at her. Tony had been unable to maneuver into another lane. They'd been hit and had rolled. Will's limp body had crushed hers.

He hadn't made it.

The loss of Will, as fresh as yesterday, slammed into her anew. Sinking into Will's pillow with a shudder, she groaned and buried her face in her hands. Dear, dear Will, who'd become her best friend after Johnny's death, was gone.

Will had been closer to her than most brothers were to their sisters. And now, because desperate circumstances had forced her to agree to marry him, she was stuck with his brother.

"It was so nice before I saw you and remembered…about Will and Tony and everything that's happened," she said. "Reality sucks," she said mournfully.

Michael's black eyes darkened, if that were possible. "I know. There's always that first moment when you wake up…before you remember. Before the horror hits you."

"I don't want to get up and face a day without them," she said. "I don't want to be in their apartment."

"*Their* apartment?"

"I…I mean Will's apartment," she corrected quickly. "*Ours*. I don't want to remember…any of it or try to go on. It's too hard."

"Tell me about it. But we don't have any choice. We have responsibilities."

He sounded nice, almost human. But he wasn't. She had to remember that.

Michael must have grabbed her phone from the nightstand and shut off her alarm because the noise suddenly stopped.

"Do you want coffee?" he asked abruptly.

When she nodded, he vanished.

She was rubbing her eyes when he returned a few minutes later with a steaming mug. "What time is it anyway?"

When he held out the mug, she sat up straighter, causing something to fall from her shoulders.

His jacket. What was his jacket doing wrapped around her? The thought of him worrying about her and watching over her was oddly unsettling.

"It's 9:00 a.m.," he said, picking up his badly wrinkled jacket and folding it under his arm.

On a normal day she would be at the bistro, preparing for the day, but because of her injuries and the spotting, she wasn't supposed to work for a whole week. Her mother had volunteered to take over for her. So, here she was, stuck with Michael.

"I never thought I'd sleep till nine. But since I've been pregnant, it happens fairly often." How could she be talking to him in this normal way?

"You're growing a baby. I don't know much about pregnancy, but I think it wears you out." His deep voice was oddly gentle. "Think how tired little kids get. You've got to take care of yourself."

His desire to protect her for her baby's sake made her soften toward him, which was a dangerous reaction. If she wasn't careful, she'd start believing he was capable of treating her decently.

But that wasn't going to happen, and she couldn't allow herself to wish he could be different.

Last night she'd actually dreamed Michael was a nice guy. In her dream she'd been afraid, and he'd come running to comfort her.

Ridiculous fantasy. He was a ruthlessly cold money machine who believed the worst of her. He'd bedded her solely to protect his brother—and the North fortune. When she'd said she wasn't interested in Will, he'd offered to set her up as his mistress—but for a price. He saw her only as a threat or as a sexual commodity for his own pleasure.

"I've been thinking," he said. "This place is too small for the two of us."

She nodded. "And I hate it here because it reminds me of Will and Tony so much."

"Since we're stuck with each other for the next week," he said, "I think we'd both be more comfortable at my penthouse."

Her heart skittered in fear as she remembered their first wanton night together in his glamorous apartment where he'd seduced her and then broken her heart.

The last thing she wanted was to spend a week in the place where she'd experienced such devastation.

"I can't go back there. Your penthouse isn't exactly neutral ground. Besides don't tony Fifth Avenue buildings like yours have dictatorial boards? Would they approve of a woman, a nobody like me from the West Side just moving in?"

"Leave the board to me. If they exact a price, I'll pay…"

"You think you can buy anything you want."

"I can—most of the time." He stared into her eyes. "I have three floors and five bedrooms. Believe me, you'd be able to avoid me there much more easily than you would here. And vice versa."

"I suppose that does have its appeal," she agreed gloomily, hoping to wound him. For some infuriatingly illogical reason the thought that he wanted to avoid her as much as she wanted to avoid him stung.

* * *

He smiled. "For once you see reason. So, pack your bag, and we'll get the hell out of here."

She stared at the single drawer where she kept her things. "I…I can't."

"What is it now?"

"My stuff is still at my old apartment," she confessed.

When one black brow arched quizzically, she had to think fast.

"We…we got married so fast, Will was still in the process of moving things out to clear space for me." Flushing, she looked away.

The trouble with lies was that if you told one, you had to keep stacking more on top of the first. How long would it be before he discovered her secret and her house of cards came tumbling down?

"Okay, then," he said. "What do you say we do breakfast, and then we go to your place? We have to feed the baby, don't we?"

She couldn't believe she was nodding and almost smiling, or that she was agreeing so easily to move in with him, when he'd behaved so terribly last night, and would probably do so again.

She should be furious. If only she could hold on to her anger and stay on her guard around him.

"Can we eat at Chez Z, so I can see how Bijou is holding up?" she asked.

He nodded much too agreeably. How would she stand a whole week with this man? She didn't trust herself to be around him when his every nice gesture made her want to trust him again.

What if he caught her in a weak moment? What if she stupidly confided her secret? What would he force her to do then?

Four

No sooner had Bree led Michael through the doors of Chez Z than she regretted it. Not that anything particularly worrisome was going on in the intimate dining room jammed with yellow chairs and tables, and paintings of sunflowers cheerfully aflame on fire-engine red walls. It was simply that being here with Michael brought back *that* night—the one that had changed her life so irrevocably and compelled her to marry Will.

Marcie looked up from setting the tables, smiled and then went back to her work as if having her battered boss show up on the arm of a devastatingly handsome man the morning after she'd survived a fatal car wreck was nothing unusual.

Bijou rushed over to ask how Bree was feeling. After giving her a concerned once-over, her mother must have felt reassured because she thanked Michael for looking after her. Then Bijou left to check the online reservations for the day, the availability of staff and the status of a delivery that was late.

Bree didn't want to think about the first night Michael had come to Chez Z, but with his strong hand gripping her wrist, it was impossible not to. His mere touch made the bright walls squeeze closer and her breath come faster.

Again she saw him striding through the doors alone on that warm summer evening, his black eyes purposeful as he looked for her. She knew now his sole intent had been to seduce her so he could neutralize her importance to Will. But that night, fool that she'd been, she'd felt flattered that he'd sought her out and had rushed up to him with pleasure.

Will had warned her about Michael, of course, saying that he was a real bastard when it came to business and could be rude and overbearing in his dealings with family and his lovers.

"He's a coldhearted genius who ruthlessly annihilates our foes. He'll do or say anything to win. Dad said he's what our family needs in this competitive world—so he put him in charge. Even though he's adopted, we all have to answer to him. Believe me, Michael interferes in everything. He says it's because he cares, and it is. But he can be rough and difficult."

"And you don't mind?"

"I mind, but he grew up hard. He once told me he was raised by wolves, so I sort of understand. He thinks he's protecting me. He really does, and he'll destroy anybody he sees as a threat to me. He worries about any woman I get close to, so stay away from him."

"But that's ridiculous. We're just friends."

"Believe me—he won't see it that way."

Had she listened?

Despite Will's warning, when his darkly handsome brother had flirted with her at the fundraiser, she'd fallen fast and hard, maybe because he'd exuded way too much masculine power, confidence and charm for an innocent like her to resist.

And, oh, how foolishly she'd exulted when he'd walked into Chez Z looking for her. *For her,* when he could have had a gorgeous supermodel.

Tall and fit in his perfectly cut gray silk suit, his brilliant gaze and quick smile had dazzled her.

Mark, the maître d', had bowed and stepped aside when she'd rushed up to Michael, saying she'd lead him to his table.

"Hello again," he'd whispered against her ear as she picked up a menu and a wine list for him. "I wasn't sure you'd remember me."

As if any woman could forget…least of all her, who had zero experience with men like him.

"Will's brother? Even if you weren't my dearest friend's brother, how could I possibly forget *you?*" Realizing how eager she must have sounded, she'd blushed. "I—I didn't mean," she'd stammered. But she had. He was gorgeous. "Welcome to Chez Z."

His hard, sensual mouth had curved in amusement as if he considered her blushes and stammering his due. "I want a table in your section."

"I'm afraid I'm off tonight. I was just about to

leave." She felt a pang of acute disappointment at this admission. "I'm going to see a movie with a friend."

"Too bad," he said with such genuine regret her tummy flipped. "Perhaps I can tempt you into joining me for a glass of champagne." He grinned down at her gently. "If I promise to select a very good year, maybe you'll decide to go to a later show."

Bree knew she was in over her head and that she should say no and leave to meet her friend, but when he looked at her in that intimate way, she wanted to be with him too badly to deny herself. Never in her whole life had she felt so excited. Cathy would have to understand.

"I guess I could stay for one glass…if it's a very good year."

He took her hand and squeezed it. As his thumb casually stroked the inside of her palm, thrilling warmth flooded her. He laughed at her blushes. Heads turned to regard them. The feminine gazes lingered on him before resting quizzically on her.

When she called Cathy, her friend suggested they postpone the outing until later in the week, which suited Bree even better.

She'd never been with anyone like Michael. Truthfully, she hadn't dated much at all. Oh, she'd loved a boy in college, but he'd broken her heart when he'd fallen for her best friend. Others had been interested in her, but she would have been settling if she'd let any of them make love to her. So, here she was, a virgin in her twenties, flirting with a man she should have run from.

Champagne, coupled with the aromas of garlic, duck and foie gras, had heightened her senses until she'd become giddy with conceit at finding herself the companion of such a virile and attractive man.

The heady pleasure of his company, of eating and drinking with him, had quickly proved too much. Food was like an aphrodisiac to her, and she wasn't much of a drinker. One glass of champagne had led to another because she hadn't wanted him to think her an ingenue.

She couldn't get enough of the cool pale liquid that tasted so bubbly and sweet. She'd basked in Michael's teasing and flirting. Suddenly there had been only him filling the dining room. The murmur of the other diners' voices and the clatter of their plates and silverware had soon died to nothing.

Soon she'd forgotten her shyness and her amazement that such a stunning man was interested in her. With such chemistry between them, of course he was interested, she'd told herself, as she'd allowed him to draw her out.

When he leaned across the table, questioning her as if he found her fascinating, she'd told him all about her brother, Z, and about the strong-minded Bijou, who had adored Z more than anyone or anything in the world. Next Bree told him about the rest of her colorful family who had supported Z in his efforts to garner fame and respect with his cooking skills.

When their frogs' legs came, Michael picked one up with his fingers, and she watched him eat it. She picked up her own frog leg and nibbled at the rich, succulent flesh as gracefully as she could. He smiled when she sucked at the juice dripping down one of her fingertips. At the same moment they both dipped their fingers into the bowl of warm water tartly scented with lemon. When their fingers accidentally touched, a hot dart of excitement made her tummy turn over.

"I wanted to go into publishing," she said, quickly yanking her hand from the bowl. "To be an editor, but the family needed me here to help Z, who was bringing us all such glory. I couldn't resist them even if I always felt a little lost and colorless around all of them. They are all people of such grand passions and ambitions."

"Don't sell yourself short," he murmured.

When he looked at her, she felt alive, special— every bit as exciting as her relatives. It was a new and heady experience.

"I'm a book person. They love being center stage. They love the television shows shot in the bistro's kitchen. But Z left me the bistro, maybe because I shared his passion for food and was the most faithful about showing up whenever he had an emergency. Ironically, my exciting family works for dull me now."

"You are not dull. Far from it. Z must have realized you cared for the bistro."

Maybe she hadn't known how much she loved it until Z was gone and he'd left it to her. Michael had a point. She did care. She didn't want to lose the bistro and all Z and her family had worked for.

"Well, I'm not doing well in business, so dull or not, I'm in trouble with them for failing Z."

Michael picked up another frog leg. "Can't you quit? This wasn't your dream."

"But it is now," she said, realizing for the first time it was true. "The bistro means so much to all of them…and yes, to me. Investors, family, friends—they've sunk money into the restaurant. It's not just about a livelihood. It's about respect and family honor. It's for Z…and all the people I love. I'll do anything to save it. *Anything.*"

His eyes had darkened. "But what about you? Are you sure this is what you want?"

"It wasn't at first, but it is now."

"I envy you, having a family, a real family, and the goal to help them."

She paused. "I'm sorry. I shouldn't have gone on like that. I've done all the talking. You know, I don't normally do this."

"Do what?"

Once more he took her hand and turned it over in his, and again she felt the sharp sizzle of sensual excitement.

"*This.* I don't date much. I don't have the time

right now. I'm sure you'd have more fun with some other girl…I mean, some other woman."

"You're very wrong." When he ran his thumb over her wrist, she gasped.

His eyes lit up, and she wondered if he sensed the intensity of her response.

"Don't apologize for being who you are," he whispered. "I like you. I came here because I wanted to get to know you better."

"Why?"

"I think you know why."

Did he feel something, too?

As he continued to run his thumb over her wrist and the inside of her palm, the hot current of desire throbbed with an ever greater force.

"Will said you're adopted."

A shadow passed over his face and his eyes grew bleak before he looked down.

She felt so stupid. Why, oh, why had she said that?

"Yes. I'm adopted." Then he was silent so long she grew uncomfortable.

"I'm sorry. I shouldn't have pried."

"No, it's okay. It's not something I talk about often, but I want to talk to you. I grew up poor.

Poor enough to know what it feels like to be nothing."

"I'm sure you were never nothing."

"Well, I felt like I was. My father, who worked in a refinery in Baytown, died when I was a baby. So, I never knew him. My mother was a masseuse and earned just enough for us to scrape by. She had boyfriends. Too many boyfriends. I didn't like them or the gifts they gave me to bribe me into accepting them. I was in the third grade when I got my first job—on the docks. Not long after that I bought a used lawn mower and started mowing lawns. I had to put myself through junior college and the University of Houston. My life was tough until my mother married Jacob North."

"How in the world did she meet him?"

"He was a client. I was nineteen and just out of college when they married. I asked him for a job, and he hired me as a stockbroker. I didn't know much back then, but I guess he saw something in me because he took me under his wing.

"With his help I advanced rapidly, which a lot of people resented, including most of his family who disliked my mother. Right before my mother died, perhaps to please her, Jacob adopted me legally—because he said he needed some-body strong he could trust to run his businesses and look after the family interests. He said Will, his only son, was too weak because he'd been spoiled. Strangely, Will, who had no interest in the business, took to me in a brotherly way, and I took to him.

"When Jacob died, Will was all I had. The rest of the Norths tried to get rid of me. They sued, tried to break Jacob's will—but they lost—big-time." His grim expression should have warned her.

"At least they're not blood kin, so there's a rea-son you don't fit in."

He'd smiled and pressed her slim fingers tightly. "Except for Will, I feel like I've been alone my whole life."

"That's sad."

"It's just the way things are."

When he'd drawn her closer, she'd felt pow-erfully connected to him when he'd said, "It's a little hard for me to trust anyone."

Why hadn't she *listened*? Too late she'd learned the man annihilated those he didn't trust.

The waiter had come, and they'd elected to

share crème brûlée and raspberries. The combined flavors of caramelized sugar, crème and tart berries had proved to be sheer perfection. Looking back, she couldn't believe she'd let Michael spoon-feed her. The memory of how warmly she'd felt toward him that night, of how deftly he'd used the sensual delight of food to seduce her, chilled her. Now she knew his interest in her had been based solely on his desire to destroy his brother's feelings for her.

Pushing back from the excruciating memories, she stiffened and marched ahead of him toward the kitchen. Even though it was still too early for lunch, her mother had already done most of the prep work, so the rich aroma of sautéed onions and garlic and other herbs flown in from Provence lingered in the air.

"I'll make you a soufflé," she said.

"You don't have to."

"Cooking relaxes me." Better than that, it would distract her from him and the reality that she was moving in with him.

She put on her apron and took four eggs out of the refrigerator while he wandered about, opening her drawers and investigating her cupboards.

Just when she was about to object to his nosiness and tell him not to touch anything, his phone rang. Instantly, he was all business as he left the kitchen to discuss stock trades and a real-estate project in Mumbai.

He didn't return until she told him the soufflé was done. Then they sat down together to enjoy it with warm, buttery croissants thick with fresh, homemade raspberry jam and rich black coffee.

As always the lush flavors of even such simple fare put her in a better humor—which meant, she'd better be on her guard. She was eating with him again.

"Thanks for letting me come here," Bree said as he sank his fork into her luscious soufflé. "I needed to see that Marcie and Bijou have everything under control."

"Where's your chef and waitstaff?"

"Bijou's here. Mark's running late because he has some family issues, but he'll be here in a few minutes to cook. We do a lot of takeout orders, and we don't need waiters for that."

"Your mother can cook?"

"Yes…and no. She loves to cook, so she cooks. But… *no!* Z and I were lucky to survive her cooking. Some of her guests were once hauled away from our house in ambulances after a family dinner when I was a child. We used to watch her in the kitchen, so we'd know what dishes to avoid."

"You're kidding."

"I wish. She used to throw anything that was about to spoil into a casserole or soup and then invite people over."

He laughed.

"We only let her start working here when she promised not to cook. Since Z died, she says she feels his spirit here. We need her, and when she's busy helping us hold Z's dream together, she feels better. Z was her favorite, you see."

"And you know this how?"

She wasn't about to tell him *she* was the reason her parents had felt obliged to marry, or that her mother had blamed Bree for the loss of her career as a concert pianist as well for her unhappy marriage.

Instead Bree said, "Z was their long-awaited son. The only thing my parents agreed on was how perfect Z was and how much they loved him. After he was born, I sort of ceased to exist."

There was a bread crumb on his lower lip. She

clenched her fingers to resist the impulse to brush it away.

"Did you hate him for that?" Michael licked his lips, and the tempting bread crumb vanished.

Just the opposite. She'd felt relieved. "Z was just always so gifted, so charming and confident. He looked up to me and adored me, so how could I hate him?"

"So, when you were younger, you wanted to be an editor."

She wished she hadn't told him that, wished that he hadn't asked her so many personal questions. Her secret longings were none of his business. But talking to him like this touched her somehow, made her think that if they tried, they could have a normal relationship.

Unable to resist opening up to him, she began to babble. "I loved reading. Stories offered a safe escape from our family dramas. I wanted to do my own thing, though I hadn't figured out what that was. But when Z became famous and had to go shoot shows in foreign lands or do book tours, he needed someone to run the restaurant, and he asked me. None of us could ever say no to Z. Mother would have helped, too, but she broke her hip and was down for six months.

"The busier Z became, the more he needed me here. And I liked being needed. Unfortunately, he died at a very bad time for the business. He'd just expanded and taken on a lot of new investors."

"Like Will," Michael said in a grim tone that made her wish she'd avoided that topic.

"Will was already an investor." She took a bite of soufflé before continuing. "The restaurant is saddled with debt. If I fail, my family will never forgive me any more than I could forgive myself. To them, closing Chez Z would be the end of Z's dream. For them, he's still alive here, you see. I feel the same way."

"I know a thing or two about dealing with family issues and business," Michael muttered as he sank his fork into the airy perfection of her soufflé again. "It's rarely easy."

"But I've got to make it work, now more than ever, and not just for my family. I need to pay off the debt and earn a decent income so I can support my baby."

"Your baby's a North. You must know you

won't have to worry about money. You're Will's widow. I'll take care of you."

"Do you think that, knowing what you think of me, I want to be dependent on you or the illustrious North money?"

His eyes hardened. "Will's dead and you're his pregnant widow. We're stuck with each other whether we like it or not."

With a coldly withering glance, he shut down on her.

He was impossibly controlling. How would she endure living with him for a week? He was an arrogant beast who thought awful things about her and was determined to control her life and her child's. Why the hell had she cooked anything for him? Why had she talked to him, told him about her family, shared her dreams?

Steamed, more at herself than at him, she stood up. Just as he was about to sink his fork into her soufflé again, she grabbed his plate.

"Hey!" he cried.

At his yelp of dismay, she grinned wickedly. When he leaped to his feet, she whirled and scraped the last of his soufflé into the sink. While he sulked, she turned on the faucet to wash it down the drain.

"That was cold," he said.

"You deserved it. We've wasted enough time on idle chitchat. I have a bistro to run. Why don't I pack, so I can get back here?"

"The doctor said you're to take the week off."

"I will. I'll just sit around here and supervise, juggle a few bills."

"The hell you will. If you think I'm going to let you stress yourself and endanger your baby just because you're stubborn, you don't know me at all."

"Look—you stress me out more than anyone or anything here ever could. I need a break from you. Okay? The last thing I need is a bullying babysitter. Don't you have an empire to run, or someone else to boss around?"

"I have quite a lot to do—as a matter of fact—but nothing matters to me more than Will's child."

"The North heir."

"*My* heir."

"Exactly," she whispered. She felt her stomach twist. "The only reason your heir matters is because he stands to inherit your precious fortune. Money is all you care about."

"You know me so well."

As Michael's gaze followed the steep, Victorian staircase up several stories into the gloom, he heard Bree struggling to get her key out of the heavy interior door that had closed behind them.

When she caught up with him, he whirled on her. "You are not climbing these stairs."

"I promise, I'll take it very slowly."

"Not in your condition! Your doctor said no to subways because of all the stairs, remember?"

"I don't remember all that."

"Well, I do, so you're to sit down on the stairs and make me an itemized list of everything you'll need for next week."

"Michael, it will be so much easier if I just go upstairs and grab—"

"You're going to give me your key, and wait here while I go up and pack for you."

"You couldn't possibly find—"

"I run an empire, remember."

"Hey, maybe I don't want you going through my things."

"You prefer to risk the baby?"

"You're making me feel like a child."

"The sooner you stop acting like one and start writing that list, the sooner we get out of here." He pulled a pen and a pad out of his pocket.

Sulkily she sat down and scribbled out a list. Then she told him that she hid her key outside her door in the bowl of potpourri. As he climbed the stairs, she dutifully stayed where she was.

Three Victorian flights were more like five modern flights, he thought as he let himself into her apartment. It was tinier, messier and much shabbier than he'd imagined for someone who had such a flair for color. He had to call her cell to ask her where her duffel bag might be when it wasn't in its proper place. Once he found it, he charged into her bathroom and pulled panties and bras and a transparent nightgown off hooks where they'd been drying. Next he scooped up toiletries and a large bottle of prenatal vitamins. Then he made his way to her bedroom so he could rummage in her chest of drawers and closet.

With an eye for what he thought would look best on her, he chose several outfits and pairs of shoes. When he was through packing he even watered her plants, a task she'd forgotten to put on her list.

"You're very bossy," she said after he'd rejoined her at the bottom of the stairs and she'd checked the contents of her duffel bag.

"I get that a lot. Mind if I take that as a compliment?"

"No. And you're fast. What you picked out... will do."

"That last's definitely a compliment."

"You're grasping at straws."

"With you, I have to. So—how come you didn't have a single picture of Will in your apartment?"

She paled. "They...they're all on my computer. I needed to print one and frame it. I just hadn't gotten around to it, I guess."

When she lowered her eyes, he sensed there was more, way more.

But what? What was she hiding?

Michael stared at his lawyer before flipping another page of the legal document in disgust. What had he expected?

Feeling acute betrayal on behalf of his trusting brother, Michael flung the papers down onto his desk.

Nothing like a legal contract in black-and-white to spell out the truth.

No doubt about it, just like his own ex-wife Anya, Bree's sole motive for marrying Will had been getting her hands on his money.

"You're saying the day Will married Bree, *on his wedding day,* he signed documents to set up a million-dollar trust fund to care for her baby? And his new bride was with him in this office when he did it? She cosigned?"

His attorney ran a hand through his shock of silver hair and then nodded. "I wasn't there when they came in, but that's her notarized signature. They had new wills drawn up, as well."

When inspired, a conniver like her sure worked fast.

"You knew about all this, and you didn't tell me?"

"I didn't draft the documents myself. You were still dealing with that mess in Shanghai when Will told me he'd hired an independent attorney who would be sending the documents over for me to review before Will and his bride signed them."

"Can we break them?"

"You can take anything to court, but if she puts up a fight, which she probably will, it will cost you more than it's worth," Roger said. "I don't have to tell you that family lawsuits are very unpleasant emotionally as well as financially. When I expressed my concerns about these documents, Will made it very clear that this was what he wanted. In fact, he insisted that I promise to tell you that very thing if anything should happen to him. He seemed very anxious to take care of his child."

"He mentioned me, did he?"

"He did. As for the new will, he left the bulk of his estate to his friend Tony. But in the event of Tony predeceasing him, which is what has happened, you still get everything as in his old will."

Now that was odd. Michael would have thought a man anxious enough to sign his will on his wedding day would have left his brand-new wife everything.

"Except Bree gets her million dollars," Michael said.

"Not exactly. He left her nothing. She's merely the trustee of her baby's fund."

"Which means," Michael said, "that she can do exactly what she wants with the money."

"There will be a second million deposited into the trust when the baby's a month old."

"Thanks for clarifying where things stand," Michael said coldly.

"Anytime. Is there anything else I can do for you?"

"Do you know how much my brother had sunk into Chez Z?"

"I have it here." Roger handed him another document. "My best guess is, he'd given her close to a quarter of a million dollars."

Michael whistled as he studied the document. "Anything else?"

Michael shook his head. "I can't thank you enough for coming by."

When the other man stood, Michael arose and extended his hand. He didn't sit down again until the older man shut the door behind him.

Bree made Will sign the documents on their wedding day. *On their wedding day.* And she'd called Michael cold.

On top of the will, his brother had given her bistro nearly a quarter of a million dollars.

Michael found the whole situation oddly disturbing. Why had his brother left everything to Tony, a man he'd never even bothered to introduce to Michael or to the rest of his family, instead of to his new wife? And how had Bree felt about that?

Still puzzled by the documents, Michael buzzed Eden, his secretary, who filled him in on his various meetings for the day. Before ending their conference, she reminded him that he was having drinks at a midtown bar with a Mr. Todd Chase at 6:00 p.m.

"Oh, that's right. Todd."

"Who's Todd?" she asked.

"An old friend from the University of Houston," Michael said. "I completely forgot he was in town." Todd had taken a job as the CEO of a huge investment-banking firm that needed a genius at the helm, and Michael had invited him for drinks to celebrate.

"You had me make a notation that he's bringing his wife, and you're taking a date. Someone named Natalia."

Damn. The last person he felt like dealing with was Natalia. Although she was beautiful, she was extremely high-maintenance. A model, she always made sure the media knew her every move. He'd seen her a couple of times before he'd left for Shanghai, mostly to send Bree a message that he was through with her.

He'd forgotten all about his "date" with Natalia tonight. Knowing her, she'd have a media event planned.

"Do you want me to call and remind her for you?" Eden asked.

"No." There'd be hell to pay with the needy, supersensitive Natalia if he didn't make the call himself—especially since he hadn't been in touch with her for nearly a month.

Even though she was one of the world's most beautiful and celebrated women, she was riddled with self-doubt. A perfectionist, she saw only her imperfections and needed vast amounts of reassurance. Strangely, disillusioned as he was with what he'd discovered today, he would have much preferred to go home early to Bree.

Bree didn't do helpless well, so she felt guilty doing nothing as she sat in her tiny office amid piles of paper she very badly needed to organize, one eye on the nightly news and the other on Bijou and their undermanned kitchen staff. Several people had begged to be off tonight, so Bijou was dashing about shouting orders and screaming ineffectively at the waiters and prep cooks.

The closer it got to the dinner hour, the more pressured Bree felt to help. But she had promised Michael she'd go to his place at 6:30 sharp. She knew that was the bistro's busiest time, and didn't want to be tempted to pitch in. Glancing at her watch, she realized she'd be late if she didn't leave immediately.

Just as she was about to grab her purse and turn off the television, Michael's tall, dark image blazed on the screen. He strode out of one of the city's flashiest hotels with a beautiful blonde dressed in a sheath of skintight silver who smiled as reporters swarmed them.

While the newscaster babbled excitedly about Natalia's seven-figure contract with a major cosmetics company and Michael's multigazillion-dollar project in Shanghai, Bree couldn't take her eyes off the sexy supermodel, whose hands were all over Michael.

Bree turned the television off and flung the

remote aside so roughly it smashed against her desk, causing its back to pop open and its batteries to spill out.

She caught them before they hit the floor. With shaking fingers she grabbed the remote and stuffed the little suckers back inside.

She didn't care who Michael dated...or how damn beautiful the woman was. He was nothing to her, nothing other than her bossy brother-in-law who'd used her doctors to bully her into moving in with him so he could run her life for the rest of this week.

He was nothing to her.

He's the father of my unborn child.

That was an unfortunate fact she would have preferred to forget.

No way was she going back to Michael's stuffy building and endure the snooty stares of his doorman and then sit in her suite behind his kitchen all alone while he was with the incredibly beautiful, immensely successful Natalia. No way. She'd stay where she was, with people who loved her and approved of her.

Just because he was her brother-in-law and a North, just because he was immensely wealthy and lived in a palatial building on Fifth Avenue, just because he was the father of her baby didn't mean he had the right to dictate to her.

He would have to earn that right.

It was well after 8:00 p.m. when Michael let himself into his dark penthouse. He'd worked with a vengeance at the office and had been five minutes late to pick up Natalia. Then she'd embarrassed him by sulking in front of Todd at the bar because he hadn't called or texted or sent flowers during the past month. When he hadn't invited her to dinner after they'd said goodbye to Todd and his wife, she'd thrown a fit.

Unfortunately, Michael had been so exhausted from his sleepless night in that chair beside Bree's bed and his long day at work, he'd exploded.

Forgetting how sensitive she was to even the slightest criticism, he'd said something about beauty, even hers, being impermanent and had advised her to let him or someone like him invest her money for her.

"My money! Is that all you care about? You don't think my beauty will last. Are you saying you don't love me, either?"

When he hadn't argued that point, she'd puffed up in hurt and indignation and slapped him. "You don't love me!"

"You don't love me, either."

"Why, oh, why does everybody hate me?"

Then Natalia had broken up with him.

She was such a child. He'd hurt her, and he hadn't meant to. Tomorrow he'd send her a note apologizing and proclaiming her beauty along with roses and a parting gift.

Okay—so he was buying her off.

But the only good thing that had come out of their unpleasant night together was that she'd taken his mind off Bree and Will for a little while.

Still, no matter what had happened today or what he'd found out about Bree, she was injured and pregnant and he'd sworn he'd take care of her and the baby.

So here he was, home early to check on a house-guest he would have preferred to strangle.

He removed his jacket and threw it on a chair. Crossing his great room, he went to the bar where he poured himself a single shot of vodka. As he bolted it, the silence of the immense room ate at him.

Earlier, before he'd left for the office, Bree had his stereo going as well as her television because she said his penthouse felt like a tomb.

Where the hell was she?

He needed a night's sleep to calm down from the attorney's news. The last thing he wanted to do was deal with Bree and risk more feminine drama, but he strode across the living room, down the hall and past his vast kitchen until he reached the guest suite.

The space was on the lower floor and had originally been designed as a maid's quarters. Since he didn't have a live-in maid, and since Bree had a thing against elevators and he had a thing against her climbing stairs in her delicate condition, he'd suggested she use the suite.

He was about to raise his hand to knock when he realized her door was ajar. Slightly alarmed, he pushed it open.

Her suite was dark. Flipping on the lights, he tore through the rooms, calling her name, first in anger, then in mounting concern.

Her duffel bag was open. Colorful, silky clothes and sparkly costume jewelry that she hadn't bothered to put away spilled onto the floor. Lacy bras and panties littered the top of the dresser. It didn't take long to determine she was out or to figure out where she probably was—Chez Z.

Damn it. She had a baby to think about. What didn't she get about her condition and the gravity of her injuries?

Did she want to lose Will's baby?

Slamming his glass down, he spun on his heel and tore out of his penthouse.

Five

When Michael didn't see Bree in the noisy, crowded dining room of Chez Z, he found Bijou, who was pouring ice water into stemmed glasses.

"Is she still here?"

Bijou's brows shot upward. "I told her to go home an hour ago, but she's in a mood."

"In a mood?"

"Everybody says she's super-dedicated to saving Z's restaurant for the family and the investors, but I call it stubborn. Still, she did take it easy all day…until this evening…around 6:30. I don't know what set her off. I told her to go home. When she was obstinate, I thought about calling you, but I misplaced your business card. And then things got busy."

He gave Bijou another business card for future reference. "Where is she now?"

"We had several plates returned to the kitchen because the scallops were soggy, so she's in the back teaching Mark how to dry scallops properly before he sautés them so they won't taste as if they've been steamed. The poor thing's nearly dead on her feet, but will she listen?"

Dead on her feet.

A pang of sympathy shot through him. Then he grew angrier. Whose fault was it, if she was tired?

Irritated, he swept past Bijou, banging through the kitchen doors in his impatience to find her.

When a startled Bree looked up, her eyes blank and shadowed with exhaustion, another wave of concern hit him.

"You're coming home with me now," Michael said.

"Your penthouse in that stuffy building is so not home."

"I'm not here to play word games," Michael said firmly.

She turned her back on him and faced the line of people in white behind her. "Ignore him. Don't let him break your concentration."

"If you don't get your purse and whatever else you think you need tonight in two seconds flat and come with me, I swear I'm going to pick you up and carry you out of here."

She whirled. "Just because you think you rule the world, and you practically do, you aren't the only one who has a job to do, you know. I have one, too."

"This isn't about our work. You're pregnant. You're the only survivor from a wreck that killed three people yesterday. You were injured."

"Minimally. I'm young and strong."

"Young and strong? You're exhausted and grieving. A corpse has more color and life than you do."

"Your heir is perfectly safe," she said.

"Step away from that stove," he ordered.

"He's right. Go on home, darlin'," Mark said behind her. "We've got your back. I swear. We won't let you down."

With Mark's betrayal, the last spark of resistance in her eyes dulled. "Okay," she whispered wearily to Mark, and then to Michael she said, "You win. I'm coming. Just don't touch me. Don't you dare put a hand on me or try to pick me up."

Although she was trying to stand up to him, she looked like she was about to shatter.

"Wouldn't dream of it," he drawled softly.

He felt close to some edge himself, dangerously out of control. Why was it that only she affected him like this?

It was a beautiful night. The moon was big, the air crisp. Not that either of them was enjoying the loveliness of the black velvet sky lit by starlight.

No, the air in the dark interior of his silver Mercedes fairly crackled with white-hot tension as Michael whipped through the crowded streets. He hadn't spoken to her since they'd left the restaurant, and he was driving so fast, Bree was almost afraid to say anything for fear of distracting him. His hands clenched the wheel. His eyes narrowed as he focused on the flying vehicles on all sides of them and the changing traffic signals ahead.

Suddenly the silence felt so thick and smothering she couldn't breathe. Reaching forward, she turned on his radio, moving the dial instinctively until she found hard rock, hoping the heavy beat would make it impossible for her to think about Michael's pulsing fury.

With a hard jerk of his wrist, he switched the radio off.

"So—do you want to talk to me or not?" she said after a long interval of unendurable, hostile silence.

"No. I just prefer silence to your insane music."

"Well, I find your bullying and your rage oppressive."

"Deal with it—since you're the cause of it."

"You didn't need to drive all this way to get me, you know. You could have called me or something."

"Right," he growled. "And just like that, you would have come running."

Glad she'd goaded him, she fought not to smile.

The big silver car shot through the dark like a missile, narrowly missing a biker, who shot the finger at them.

When she heaved in a breath and clenched her door, she realized how shaken she must still be from the accident.

"Hey, shouldn't you slow down before you kill us or some innocent courier?"

"You're so self-destructive I'm surprised you care," he said, but after glancing at her, he lifted his foot off the accelerator fractionally.

"Oh, because if I don't do exactly what you say, I'm self-destructive?" she persisted, trying to ignore her fear of the other cars.

"How long were you at the bistro?"

"All day."

"Exactly." His single word punched the air with such force it took all her courage to dare a shocked glance at his broad-shouldered profile.

"Quit sulking. Everybody works better if I'm there," she said. "I owe a lot of people a lot of money. I don't want to let them down."

"Right—you're so *dedicated.*"

His scowl told her he was still furious.

"What's the matter with you? I thought you were on a date, enjoying yourself with that model. Having the time of your life."

"*What?*" The single word ripped into her like an explosion.

Before she knew what he was doing, he'd jerked the car across two lanes, to the curb, amid a barrage of blaring horns. Once they stopped, he engaged his warning lights.

"What's wrong with you?" she cried.

"*You!* Do you think I want you in my life? Want you haunting my every thought? I drove myself all day at the office in the hope I could forget about you and the way you used your charm to blindside my brother. The poor fool took off his seat belt to save you. *He's dead because of you!*"

His cruel words hit their intended mark. She'd tormented herself with the same thought, but she swallowed tightly and held her head high.

"Hey," she said, "while I was in my office—resting *obediently*—who should I see but you? On TV. With one of the world's most beautiful women. Natalia Somebody Or Other."

"I had a late business meeting. She was my date."

"Right. Well, you didn't look the least bit haunted to me. You weren't going to be at your penthouse, so why should I go over there and sit around all by myself dwelling on Will and Tony when you were out having fun?"

"Fun? You think you know everything about me, do you?"

"I know you want to be seen with women like her, that you date them or collect them…probably just to enhance your image because you don't have a heart."

"Collect them? No heart? So—now I'm inhuman, too?"

"I know that the only reason you slept with me was to make Will hate me because you were protecting his precious money…and your own."

When he thought about the trust fund she'd acquired the day of her marriage, her holier-than-thou attitude grew intolerable.

"With sharks like you out there, someone had to protect it."

"See—you don't care about me at all! Why are you so concerned about what I'm doing?"

"*I don't care?* You think I don't care?" He felt out of control, on dangerous ground, but he couldn't back down. *He cared too much.* That was the problem.

"I felt lost and miserable. The restaurant took my mind off things. So what if I didn't go to your penthouse? You had Natalia to distract you, didn't you?"

"Shut up. Forget Natalia. She means nothing to me."

"Well, she had her hands all over you, and you seemed to be eating it up."

"You don't know anything about me. About what I feel."

"What do you feel then?"

"Disappointment. Disillusionment…that you're as bad as I believed you to be."

"Oh…." She *so* didn't like him.

Then why did his assessment crush her?

Unsnapping his seat belt and then hers, he yanked her toward him roughly.

"Quit it! I don't want to be manhandled by someone who dislikes me."

"I wish I disliked you," he muttered. "Even though I know what you are, on some level I fell for the sweet innocent you pretended to be that first night and can't get her out my head."

"The last thing I want to think about is that night!" When she balled her hands and pushed against his massive chest, his mouth closed over hers.

"I don't want to kiss you when you're angry like this, when you say such awful things," she whispered as his hard, determined lips took hers again. "Don't do this."

His breath came in harsh rasps. "I don't want Natalia, you little fool," he said. His tongue pushed inside her mouth. "I want you," he said. "In spite of everything that's hard and cold about you, I want you." He kissed her again.

Beneath his anger, Bree felt the fierce desire inside him. Natalia or no Natalia, he was as lonely as Bree was and driven by needs he fought but couldn't deny.

It was as if they were both two lost creatures hemmed in by this crowded city where neither could find a haven anywhere but with each other. Which was ridiculous. She wasn't lost; she had a family. And he hated her. He was a heartless money machine who dated gorgeous supermodels for show. She didn't even like him.

So why was his mouth fused to hers, and why had she stopped fighting?

Why was he kissing her like a man who would die if he couldn't have her?

Her hurt over his poor opinion of her, her hurt over Natalia, was forgotten. Dazed, her arms closed around his neck, and she pulled him closer, communicating with her seeking lips and tongue that she wanted him as desperately as he wanted her.

He kissed her until she couldn't breathe. Until his anger dissolved, and his kisses grew sweeter. Then his lips moved lingeringly down her throat.

After an infinite time of shared kisses and feverishly whispered love words passed between them, he dragged his mouth from hers and stared at her in the dark. Again, the intensity in his gaze communicated his need. The same wildness that pulsed in his blood, pulsed in hers. Confused, she didn't think she'd ever seen so much misery, shock or passion in anyone's eyes as she saw in his.

How could he, of all people, blow away everything she knew to be sensible and logical and make her want him with every fiber of her being?

What if he's not as bad as I thought or as bad as he thinks he is? He came after me tonight, didn't he? He came after me because he cares.

If you think that, you're a fool—you never want to see the truth about people when your heart's involved.

But my heart's not involved. I won't let it be.

She didn't know what to say or do. Apparently neither did he. Without offering an apology or explanation, he turned off the warning lights, snapped on his seat belt and ordered her to fasten hers. Too shaken by what had happened to protest, she obeyed him.

They drove through a tangle of Manhattan traffic, most of it jostling taxicabs, in tense silence until they reached Fifth Avenue. Then, even as he was racing around the front of his Mercedes to open her door, she jumped out. Slamming it, she stalked silently past him and his uniformed doorman, although she did blush when the man's eyebrows rose in what she imagined to be disapproval.

She'd forgotten how impossibly stuffy Michael's building was with its rules that had been dreamed up for decades—to keep out the wrong *elements*.

Michael caught up to her at the elevator. "Behave," he whispered, "at least, while we're in the lobby."

Ignoring the splendor of marble and chandeliers, she shut her eyes and swallowed a deep breath. When she opened her eyes she focused on the bronze elevator doors.

Wrong move.

Elevators! Why did he *have* to live in a penthouse? Why had she ever agreed to stay here? Even for one night?

Her wild eyes must have betrayed her fear because he said, "You ever going to tell me why you're scared of elevators?"

"Maybe someday," she said trying to make her voice light.

After her cousin Jeremy had locked her in that dark closet for hours, she'd disliked all closed spaces, but a second childhood experience had further refined her phobia so that elevators had become her number one terror.

When her mother had taken Bree along to sign a paper at her attorney's office, Bijou had gotten off on the attorney's floor while talking to another woman. Bree had dropped a bunny and rushed back inside the elevator for it. Unfortunately, the doors had closed and the elevator had whooshed upward. She'd become too hysterical to punch the buttons, and the thing hadn't stopped until she'd reached the top floor. By then she'd been lost and alone and terrified she'd never find her mother.

Michael must have sensed her desire to bolt when the elevator doors opened because his hand closed gently over her elbow and he nudged her inside. When the bronze doors shut them inside, she clenched her hands and shut her eyes and tried not to think that they were shooting up dozens and dozens of stories in a closed box at rocket speed.

Sensing her growing panic as the elevator ascended, he muttered something that might have been meant to reassure her, but she felt too on edge to comprehend anything.

She didn't realize she'd begun to shake until his arms closed around her, and he drew her close to steady her. She should have fought him, but instead she clung gratefully.

Then the doors opened, and she came back to herself. Pushing free of him, she all but jumped out into his elegant hall. When he caught up with her at his door and unlocked it, she raced toward her suite and shut herself inside. Sagging against the door, she waited for her heart to slow down.

No sooner could she breathe normally than

she heard him in the kitchen, slamming cabinet doors. When the rich aroma of bacon and eggs frying and bread toasting wafted into her room, she realized that even though she'd been at the bistro, she hadn't eaten in hours.

Her stomach growled. Why couldn't he have gone upstairs so she wouldn't have to think about him out there enjoying eggs and bacon while she was trapped in here?

When he kept stomping about, she removed her phone from her purse and attached it to a set of external speakers. Soon the suite was flooded with pulsating rock. She'd shower. By then maybe he would have finished his meal and gone upstairs and she could safely raid his kitchen.

Hearing the roar of her rock music, Michael's thoughts turned to the woman in his guest suite.

Hell, why couldn't he forget the taste of her sweet mouth in the car? Forget the sharp bite of her nails digging into his back?

He wanted her, his brother's pregnant widow, this woman he'd sworn he'd protect.

But she was injured, and a gold digger, so he fought not to think of her stripping in her bathroom, showering and then slipping into her bed wearing the transparent nightgown he'd selected. Or maybe she'd wear nothing.

It drove him crazy to remember how warm and soft she'd felt curled against him that night after they'd made love. He'd wanted to hate her, but he hadn't been able to. The truth was, he'd give anything to hold her close like that again.

Who was she? The gold digger or the sweet voluptuous siren who'd enchanted him with her innocence?

Who had seduced who? He still didn't know.

Had Michael really been her first? *Had he?* Why did he care? She'd wasted no time getting herself pregnant so Will would marry her.

But Michael's questions wouldn't stop. Something was wrong with his picture of her. The pieces to the puzzle didn't fit.

Was she dedicated to the bistro for noble reasons? Or was she as low and conniving and greedy as he kept telling himself? She'd damned sure signed those documents on her wedding day. Did she kiss him in the car merely because he was rich?

Hell, she'd damn sure responded when he came on to her.

Michael's mind and emotions raged as he tore his hand through his hair. He had to get a grip.

When he finished his dinner, he rinsed his dishes and left them in the sink for Betsy Lou, his cleaning lady, who came every morning to tidy up.

Long after he'd climbed the stairs and endured a long, icy shower, he thought about Bree. Only in sleep did he have what he craved, when she came to him in his dreams and lowered her naked body over his and did everything that he desired.

Just as he was about to find his release, he heard a scream from two floors below.

Six

One minute Bree was sound asleep and happily dreaming that she was back in Michael's Mercedes wrapped in his arms as he whispered such sweet words.

Then her dream twisted, and she was shut out of his Mercedes. Standing on the sidewalk. Feeling lost and abandoned, she watched him inside his car kissing the beautiful Natalia whose slanting eyes glittered in triumph as she stared at Bree over Michael's shoulder.

Hurt washed over Bree. Thrashing against her sheets and pillows, she came awake in Michael's moonlit guest suite.

Sitting up amid tangled covers, she gave herself a minute to settle. Then she forced herself to think about her dream because she believed that dreams were a form of truthful self-talk. If she didn't think about it immediately the most telling details would recede.

She chewed on her bottom lip. The dream was worrisome. It told her that she wanted Michael even though she couldn't believe he really wanted her.

So what else was new?

As she lay there feeling frustrated and unable to sleep, a fierce craving for sardines—for anything salty and fishy—compelled her to arise, shrug into the enormous man's robe she'd found earlier in her closet and pad into his kitchen.

Remembering seeing a can of sardines sitting right by a big jar of peanut butter in the pantry, she found them easily. Smiling, she grabbed the can.

A sandwich would be good. A sandwich with mayo and pickles and maybe mustard and onions. Now that she thought about it, a white creamy cheese…Camembert. Almost tasting the rich, gooey French cheese, she headed toward his refrigerator. Her head buzzing with food fantasies, she wondered if Michael had chips, as well.

Disappointed when she found only an old onion, some cheddar and a jar of mayo but no pickles—she could never be with a man who could live without pickles—she grabbed the mayo. But as she turned to close the door the overlong sleeve of her borrowed robe snagged on the handle. The mayo jar along with the cheddar cheese and onion slipped out of her hand and smashed to jagged bits on the granite floor. Off balance, she grabbed for the counter and dropped everything else into the mess. When she moved to start picking up after herself, a shard of glass sliced into her heel and she screamed.

She froze when she saw the pool of scarlet oozing out of her torn heel. Just when she spotted his paper towels on the far side of the kitchen, a bare-chested Michael, wearing only blue pajama bottoms, stepped into the kitchen.

Why did he have to be so heart-stoppingly sexy? "Stay where you are," he ordered in that tone that made her feel gauche and then bristle defensively. His black eyes darkened dangerously at the sight of her blood as he strode toward her.

"I don't want to be a bother. I can take care of myself," she protested.

"Right," he grumbled testily as he stared at her bloody foot. "I can see that."

"I was just about to get the paper towels—"

"Do think I would risk you cutting yourself again before we even know how bad it already is?"

"I'll be fine."

"I intend to make sure of that."

Lifting her into his arms as if her weight was nothing, he crushed her against his chest as he carried her out of the kitchen and then down the hall.

Pressed so close to his hard bare flesh, she couldn't help but inhale his clean male scent. The smell brought back the night she'd spent in his arms when they'd made love. He was too virile and too sexy when he was being so nice, and she was a sucker for nice.

"Put me down," she whispered even as he headed for the stairs. "Blood is dripping behind us."

"Good thing I have stone floors and a maid coming in the morning."

"Only one maid for this place?"

"I'm not nearly as messy as you are."

Stung, maybe because she could see that about him, she rushed to her own defense. "My apartment isn't always the way it was when you saw it. I…was sort of…preoccupied last month."

"I wasn't criticizing you. I was stating a fact. Do you think I care about your apartment?"

"Put me down. Where do you think you're going? What are you doing?"

"I need to clean up your foot, and the nearest bathtub is on the second floor. Since you don't like elevators, I'm carrying you up."

"But I can handle elevators," she said testily, perversely annoyed at his thoughtfulness.

"Right." He grinned down at her. "You do them so well."

"I practice."

"How? Like one would a piano?"

Her lips twitched. She fought not to smile. "Sort of."

He wasn't nice. She didn't like him. She didn't find him amusing. He was making fun of her neurotic fear, a fear that was perfectly logical considering what had happened to her. She should be furious.

But it felt much too marvelous to be in his arms, much too nice to have him pretending that he cared.

Be careful. He's tricky. He was nice the night he seduced you. And here you are—pregnant.

As he climbed the stairs, he went more slowly at the top, and she noted with satisfaction that his breath came a little harder.

She smiled. So he was human after all.

When he reached the lovely white marble bathroom accented with gold, he helped her sit down on the edge of the tub. Kneeling, he ran his hands over her ankle before he lifted her foot and examined it.

"It's not too deep," he said as he gently removed a couple of pieces of glass. "I think I got them all. Don't watch, or this will hurt more," he said.

"What?"

"Shut your eyes. I need to make sure I got all the glass."

"Ouch," she cried when he yanked out a third sliver.

"Sorry about that. It was a little deeper than the others. But I think that's it. I'll just wash your foot now and bandage it."

She'd never imagined a man stroking her foot could make her feel so sexy, especially when she was bleeding, but apparently he could make any activity sexy.

"If you give me your first-aid kit, then I can take it from here."

"No," he snapped in that forceful tone that could so annoy her. Only it didn't annoy her now.

Turning on the water, he held his hand under the stream until it was cool enough to suit him.

"That's too cold," she cried when he stuck her foot into the flow.

But his grip on her ankle remained firm. "Hold still. Cold water helps blood clot."

"I think you just enjoy torturing me—Dr. North."

"That, too," he teased. Ignoring her, he let the icy water stream over her heel for another minute. Then he found towels. After drying her foot, he deftly applied ointment, butterfly stitches, and a bandage.

"There," he said, after he'd finished. "I don't think we need to go to the E.R."

Feeling a little chagrined, she studied her expertly bandaged foot and then the wreck they'd made of the lovely bathroom. But after the car accident, she felt truly grateful that he'd taken care of her. The last place she wanted to visit was an E.R.

"Thank you," she whispered.

"You're welcome. Now what exactly were you doing in my kitchen in the middle of the night?"

It started with a dream about you kissing Natalia, she thought. Aloud she said, "It couldn't possibly matter."

"Tell me."

For no reason at all she found herself staring at the black hair on his bare chest in fascination. "I woke up with this…er…craving."

When he turned, she couldn't resist watching the play of his muscles as he folded the towels.

Brilliance flashed in his black eyes when he glanced at her lips. "For what?"

Heat crept up her throat before she could avert her eyes. "If I tell you, you'd better not laugh at me."

With some effort he made his handsome face severe. "I won't—I promise."

"A sardine sandwich."

He struggled not to laugh, he really did, but he

couldn't help himself. The rich rumble of amusement made him seem slightly less formidable.

"You promised," she whispered.

"Well, since I broke my promise—I owe you. After all that you've gone through tonight and now my sin of laughter, you damn sure can't go back to bed without your sardine sandwich."

"It's okay. The cheese and onion are ruined, and you don't have anything else in your refrigerator. And I really have to have cheese and onions with sardines…"

"Trust me. There's more onions and cheese in Manhattan."

"It's late. I don't want to be a bother. I should let you go to bed."

"I'm making you a sardine sandwich, the sardine sandwich slathered in cheese and onions of your dreams…whether you agree to eat it or not."

She considered before she said yes. "I'm agreeing to this only because you are too obstinate to argue with. But—I'm taking the elevator down."

"You sure about that?" When he grinned, she nodded fervently. "It's only one floor. What could possibly go wrong?"

"Famous last words. So, do we go down together? Or one by one?" he asked, humoring her.

"One by one. That way if either of us gets trapped, the other can call for help."

"Right," he said. "Just for the record, there's a phone in my elevator, if you're ever caught in it alone."

"But the phone could malfunction."

"Are you always a worst-case-scenario thinker?"

"Always when it comes to elevators."

In the kitchen he cleaned up the mess, salvaging what he could, which was the can of sardines. The rest he threw in the garbage while she sat at his table and watched.

"Tell me exactly what you want on your sandwich, and I'll call my doorman."

"Can you do that? Will he do that? In the middle of the night?"

"Just tell me what you want."

"You must be impossibly spoiled."

"I pride myself on it."

When she told him the ingredients, he wrinkled his nose.

"Don't laugh at me again."

He smiled. "I believe you *are* pregnant."

He picked up his phone and made the call. When he hung up, he said, "One sardine sandwich will appear as if by magic in fifteen minutes."

Her opinion of his stuffy building and his uptight staff went up a notch.

"I've been thinking about your restaurant," he said while they waited for her sandwich. "I could help you turn it around."

She remembered he'd said that before—if she became his mistress.

"But why would you? I mean..." She frowned. "What would you want in return?"

"Nothing. You're my brother's widow. My brother sunk a quarter of a million dollars into it."

Her eyes widened. "That much? No wonder you're—"

"Didn't you know?" His voice was grim. "Really, you should know these things."

"You're right. I should have known. It was just that Z handled all that."

As he studied her, she would have given anything to be able to read his mind.

"Okay, then," she said, knowing she'd be a fool

not to let him help her. "What exactly do you have in mind?"

"For starters, I'd send over an expert in the restaurant business to evaluate what's going on. Have you ever heard of Luke Coulter?"

"The genius with seafood on TV? Who hasn't?"

Not only was Luke Coulter a successful restaurateur, he was one of New York's most renowned celebrity chefs. Z had resented that she'd been hooked on one of Luke's cooking shows.

"Z considered him a fierce rival. Bijou knows how he felt about Luke."

"Well, you're not Z, and you're in serious trouble. From what I've read, Z was not only creative, he was practical. I'm sure he'd want you to do whatever it takes to succeed. Look, I recently helped Luke restructure the financing of his latest restaurant, which, as you know, is another big hit. So he owes me a favor or two. Why don't I ask him to come over? He'll take a look at your books and your costs, watch your staff, observe how you handle them, sample your food and then give you advice. You don't have to take it—if you don't think it applies to your bistro."

Had Will really invested a quarter of a million

dollars in Chez Z? No wonder Michael thought she was out for all she could get. How much did she owe her other investors? He was right. She *should* know these things.

Fresh tension ate at her. The only thing she knew for sure was how much she didn't know.

Z had been in charge of the numbers. She had only a vague idea about her food costs and the specifics of her financial situation. She felt a bit defensive at the thought of Michael sending in an expert who might humiliate her. But what was a little humiliation? The bistro was in trouble, and things were getting worse under her management, not better. If she kept on her same path, wouldn't she keep getting the same results?

In the end she decided she owed too much money to too many people to say no. What if Luke could give her a crash course that would help her turn things around?

"Okay," she whispered, her voice low and tight. "Thanks. I'd be happy to hear what he has to say."

Not that she was happy. No, she felt scared and nervy.

Fortunately, the doorbell rang.

"Great! Your sardine sandwich is here, and it's right on time."

After Michael brought it to her, they sat down again at his kitchen table. She grew increasingly self-conscious when he smiled as she unwrapped her huge sandwich.

"Don't you want some? This really is much too big for me," she said.

He shook his head. "You're eating for two."

"I could cut it in two and share."

"That's very generous of you. But no."

"I'm absolutely ravenous."

"Enjoy."

When he didn't talk about business anymore, she began to relax. She studied her magnificent sandwich. Appetite and sensuality flooded her as she bit into the crusty bread and sardines.

"Careful," he whispered, handing her a napkin.

She munched happily, savoring the combination of tart mustard, cream cheese and fish.

A few minutes later she'd eaten all she could and was feeling sick with pleasure when she set her huge sandwich aside.

He smiled. "Had enough? Okay, then. Run along to bed. I'll tidy up."

"Why are you being so nice to me all of a sudden?" she said, feeling suspicious again.

"Maybe because you were hurt in my home. Suddenly I've been thinking maybe we should call a truce. What are we accomplishing by being so rude to each other?"

She stared at him blankly. "You started it."

"I won't argue. So, will you let me end it? What do you think—can we have a truce?"

When she hesitated, his quick, easy grin made her blood heat, made her remember the kisses in the car and the wonderful sandwich he'd ordered for her.

"Come on," he coaxed. "You're always acting like you're the one who's all heart. Show me that you're a tolerant, liberal denizen of the West Side for real."

Knowing she shouldn't let her guard down, she nodded warily as she backed out of the kitchen.

Funny, she'd felt so much safer when he'd acted as though he was dead set against her than she felt when he was helpful and friendly. Was he trying to lower her defenses so he could move in for the kill?

With some effort she recalled his ruthless reputation in business and with women, and how ruthlessly he'd treated her to protect his brother.

His feelings for her hadn't changed. If she were smart, she wouldn't let her defenses down.

Seven

"Have you got those food costs for me yet?"

Luke Coulter smiled down at her as he stepped into her office.

"Not quite. But almost. Like you said, I haven't been keeping very good records, so it's taking me a while."

"It's essential that you know what they are. You can't be fuzzy about numbers or they'll kill you."

When she handed him her notebook, which bulged with dog-eared receipts, he took the jumble and sat down.

Bree couldn't believe how easy it was to work with Luke once Bijou and everybody had warmed up to him. With his shaggy blond hair and affable smile, he seemed like a huge blond bear, albeit a friendly one—most of the time. His quick temper could be formidable.

Michael had brought Luke to the bistro three days ago. After he'd gone over her books and sampled their menu, he'd been fairly brutal with his criticism about everybody, especially her. She and her staff had been doing their best to improve so they could please him.

He'd told her she had to take control of everything—the staff and every creative and financial detail. "You can't please everybody," he'd said. "This is a job—more than a job, it's your career. Your future."

And her baby's future. Who knew if the trust fund Will had so generously set up would be enough?

Besides, Bree didn't come from a family who sat around.

"You have to account for everything you buy and sell, and to know what everything costs so you can price your menu correctly. You can't keep advancing money to all your employees the way you've been doing. Marcie's in to you for five hundred dollars."

"Her little girl's been sick."

"You can't afford to be everybody's lifeboat when the mother ship is sinking. Will you let me talk to your staff about this and establish a new policy?"

"Yes."

He'd managed to squeeze in two more tables in their back dining room, he'd revised their menu and taught her cooks several new, delicious dishes that would be easier and less costly to serve.

"This place can make it," he said as he skimmed her receipts and slashed through several marks she'd made in her notebook with his red pencil. "You have a devoted staff and a loyal clientele. You were doing fine until you lost Z, who kept a firm rein on the finances. Nobody's stealing money. Things haven't slid that far. We don't have that much to tweak."

"You have been incredibly generous with your time. I can't believe you came over right after Michael called you."

Luke's intense blue eyes met hers. "Michael let me know just how important you are to him."

New hope sent hot blood rushing to her cheeks,

but she was embarrassed that Luke might read her too accurately.

"It's not what you think. He was just trying to be helpful," she said.

"Michael is never helpful without some motive. I wouldn't underestimate his interest if I were you," Luke said. "Be careful. He's extremely focused, calculating and very, very dangerous. You're not exactly his type."

She looked away. "Right, he prefers models."

"That's not what I meant. Being a man, maybe I read him a little more clearly than you do."

"I'd rather not talk about Michael, if you don't mind."

Luke held up his hands. "Okay. We could go back and forth all day. Michael is not as fierce as he sometimes seems. He was different…before he married Anya. She made him feel as if he was worthless, made him believe no woman would want him for anything other than his wealth. Because of his past, when he felt he was nothing—he can't let those feelings go. Since he divorced her, he has concentrated single-mindedly on business and he's grown harder."

"I don't know why you're telling me this."

He laughed. "Don't you? Michael's unhappy, and you have a soft spot for people who are in trouble. Look at the way you've tolerated Mark's repeated absences even on nights when the bistro is packed or the way you've let Marcie take advantage of your generosity. Michael's like a wounded wild creature, and you want to heal him and tame him. If you aren't careful, he'll gobble you alive."

She felt her cheeks flame. He already had.

"I'm sorry." His voice was kind. "I've said too much. I've got you blushing and upset again. It's just so obvious that the two of you—"

"I'm not upset." But she was.

"Why don't we get back to these fascinating numbers before you are," he murmured drily. He pointed to a number. "Did you know you were spending this much on toothpicks?"

As Michael deftly whipped his silver Mercedes past a honking cab, he parked at the curb just in time to see Bree laughing as she walked out of Chez Z on Luke's arm.

She wore a brightly flowered pink blouse and a flounced lavender skirt. Bright beaded necklaces dangled from her neck, and her waist was sashed with a fringed orange scarf. He remembered how his doorman had smiled and then refused to meet Michael's eyes when he'd left the building with her this morning.

Michael had never seen her looking so light-hearted and happy. He frowned. Yes, he had. She'd been like that the first night he'd flirted with her at the fund-raiser, and then again *that* night at the bistro when he'd seduced her...before he'd told her the truth.

She had a beautiful smile, and he liked the way her golden eyes sparkled and her bright curls tumbled. What he didn't like was thinking that Luke had caused her special radiance.

Michael wanted Bree to look at him like that, to feel that relaxed and happy around him.

When he called out to her, she blushed and gave Luke a quick goodbye hug. Luke's broad, tanned face broke into a grin, too, as he waved at Michael before lumbering off down the crowded sidewalk.

Her eyes wary now, Bree came over to the Mercedes. When Michael opened his passenger window, she leaned down and he caught the fragrance of strawberries mingling with the rich aroma of onions a vendor was grilling on a cart.

"Ready?" he growled.

"I'll just be a minute," she said, smiling. "I need to get my purse."

A few seconds later, purple clutch in hand, she slid breathlessly into his Mercedes.

"How did it go today?" he asked as he'd asked her every day after work. He liked the way it was beginning to feel like a pleasant habit.

"Better and better. Luke's wonderful, like you said."

He knew how things were going because he talked to Luke every night. Luke liked her.

"Great," Michael replied.

"Thanks so much for asking Luke to take a look at the bistro. He's made me see all sorts of things I never saw before."

"I'm glad it's working out." He was, but at the same time, he envied her easy friendship with his friend.

"Yes. But it's been a stressful three days."

"Change is never easy."

"I'm lousy with money, but I'm determined to improve."

When he pulled into the traffic she fell silent and stared out the window.

"How did it go at the doctor's?" he asked.

"Wonderful. He cleared me. The baby's doing great. I'll be fine on my own now."

"He released you a day early, did he?"

He was relieved she was out of danger. Even so, her bright smile and quick nod darkened his mood.

"What did he say about your foot?"

"That you missed your calling, that you would have given him a run for his money if you'd gone into medicine. If we go to your place now, I can pack and be out of your hair in no time. I'm sure you think that's wonderful because you won't have to explain me to your super or your board or come down to breakfast every morning and be bombarded by hard rock anymore."

"Right."

Funny, how little the thought of peace and quiet and indulgent luxury or the approval of a bunch of nosy, uptight neighbors mattered to him.

He wanted Bree with him in his penthouse. He enjoyed her. He wanted…

What he wanted was dangerous as hell.

"Hey," he said, "I've been making the arrangements for Will's memorial, so there are a few last-minute details we need to go over together."

"Sure. We'll talk while I pack."

That would mean she'd be gone in less than an hour.

He shook his head. "I worked through lunch. Since we both have to eat, why don't I take you somewhere nearby for a quick dinner?"

It annoyed him when she argued, but he easily overrode her complaints and drove them to one of his favorite restaurants with a magical view of Central Park.

"I thought you said a quick dinner," she said as he let her out at the five-star hotel.

"I know how you love really good food."

"But you shouldn't bring me here," she protested even as they followed the maître d' into an elegant dining room accented with soft, muted colors and the glow of warm candlelight.

"Why not?"

"You said we were going to discuss the memorial arrangements."

"All the more reason we should choose an enjoyable place, don't you think?"

"But I'm not dressed properly."

"Nonsense. You look lovely."

"Like a gypsy with too many scarves and bangles."

"A truly lovely gypsy," he replied in a husky tone that was meant to coax and seduce.

This time, he knew her vivid blush, which said *don't you dare try to seduce me over a meal again,* was meant for him instead of Luke.

The waiter seated them by a window with a magnificent view. As soft music tinkled in the background, he watched her as she admired the park and the city. Why did he feel so at home in her presence and so uneasy at the thought of her moving out?

The sky was dark, and the sommelier pointed out the lightning in the far distance.

"Looks like it's going to rain," Michael said. "It may get a little chilly."

"It's that time of year," she replied.

With a smile, Michael ordered the tasting menu and asked the sommelier to bring appropriate wines for each course.

"You know I can't drink right now," she said.

"Wine looks so nice on the table."

"It's extravagant to use wine to decorate."

"You've already told me I'm spoiled. Indulge me. After all, you did agree to that truce, and it is our last night together."

He made quick work of the memorial details and settled down to enjoy her, a pleasure that began even before the waiter brought them a tiny plate with a minuscule porcini tart and other delicacies, including slim slices of lamb tucked into crisp greenery.

"An amuse-bouche, mademoiselle," the waiter said in his perfectly accented French. "*Un petit* gift from the chef."

"This is too exquisite, Michael," she said as soon as the waiter vanished. "I can't believe what I'm tasting. Lamb sorrel, chickweed and dandelion. What an imaginative combination of flavors. So rich…and yet subtle. How do they do this? I feel like I'm in a romantic forest glade."

What the hell was chickweed? He didn't care. All that mattered was that his lovely gypsy was running her tongue over her lips and shutting her eyes in pure, sensual bliss and looking so aroused it was all he could do not to reach across the table and touch her. Too bad they were in a public restaurant instead of her imaginary forest glade.

He caught himself. He knew what she was, so why did he continue to want her in his life?

Next, they had soup. Again, she noted her surprise at its originality. She couldn't stop rhapsodizing about the sharp mint of the chives mingled with the sweetness of the garlic.

"I've never had such an elegant soup made from such basic ingredients," she said in pleasure and awe. "How does he get the flavors to run so deep?"

And so it went, her attitude toward him improving with each marvel that she tasted, each course delighting her more than the last. All around them the rich fragrances of roasted ducks being carved at nearby tables and caramel sauces being drizzled over poached foie gras swirled around them.

The festive and voluptuous richness of the food seemed to make her forget her fear of him. It definitely made him forget his doubts about her.

He was so mesmerized by her sparkling eyes and quick blushes, he scarcely noted the clinks of silverware or the sounds of the other diners' muted laughter. It was as if they were the only two people in the universe.

For dessert he ordered a chocolate napoleon and she ordered warm raspberries followed by vanilla cream, which she ate with the relish of a true gourmet.

"That was all so delicious," she said dreamily as she licked the last of the cream off her spoon with the pink tip of that tongue of hers that he knew could be so wickedly clever at other erotic things.

A hot frisson of desire shot through him. God, he wanted her—wanted her to continue living with him indefinitely, wanted to sleep with her again.

Not that he gave her any indication of his feelings or intentions as he caught the waiter's eye, held up his hand and signaled for their bill.

When it was time to leave, she arose reluctantly, as if she'd enjoyed dining with him as much as he'd enjoyed her.

"That was nice. Really, really nice," she gushed. "You shouldn't have done it, but thank you so much."

He nodded. "I assure you. It was my pleasure."

She was still blushing when the valet brought his car around and Michael helped her slide into the cocoon of the plush, black leather interior.

Her heart beat much too fast as they stepped outside into the damp coolness of the rainy night. She shouldn't trust him. The meal, which had been too fantastic for words, combined with his attentive, amusing companionship, had her in a dangerously aroused mood. Had he remembered how their first shared meal had primed her senses in the same way? All night his gaze had been so dark and intense, she burned. Had he planned tonight's dinner tonight for some underhanded reason?

She, who never wanted to believe the worst of anyone—not even him—didn't want to think that. He'd been nicer since she'd injured her foot, treating her almost as if he was her friend. He was helping her with the bistro, wasn't he? Maybe he was beginning to like her a little. She felt a dangerous hunger to finish this night of sensual delights in his bed.

Stupid idea. She couldn't let him know.

He helped her into his sleek Mercedes and then

slid behind the wheel. When she dared a glance at him, their eyes met and she felt the familiar sizzle. Then her gaze fell to his tight mouth and lingered as she remembered the erotic pleasures those lips were capable of giving her.

Realizing how desperately she longed for him to kiss her, she tore her gaze away and forced herself to focus on the pedestrians that streamed past them on the sidewalks in an endless, colorful flood.

Closing her eyes, she tried to settle down as the big silver car—its tires hissing, its windshield wipers slashing—raced through the rain.

Why had she told him the doctor had released her early? If she hadn't told him, she could have stayed another night. Then maybe she wouldn't feel this perverse urgency, this sense that it might be her last chance to be with him….

When she nervously began to chew on a fingernail, he seized her hand, brought it to his lips and blew a warm breath over her skin.

"Don't!" he admonished. "Your hands are too pretty to ruin."

She yanked the offending hand free and sat on it as stubbornly as a guilty child. All the while, savage, inexplicable desire for him pulsed inside her like a jungle drum. He didn't look at her or speak again, but she was afraid he read her mind because suddenly the air between them grew so tense it sparked.

She wanted him—this impossible, difficult man, who was the secret father of her precious, unborn child. Despite his critical opinion of her and all the other reasons she shouldn't want him, what she wanted, more than anything, was another taste of the forbidden in his bed.

She did *not* have to surrender to temptation.

She *would not* surrender to it. After spending the past few days with him, her feelings now ran deeper. She was pregnant with his child. If he insulted her this time, the hurt would be even more unbearable than before.

What she *would* do was throw her belongings in her duffel bag and march out of his penthouse with her head held high.

Geography, if not willpower, would save her from herself and this much-too-sexy man.

But she'd forgotten about his elevator.

Eight

Even before the doors of the elevator trapped her inside a tiny box with Michael, her heart was drumming madly in her throat. Then the cage jerked, throwing her against him. She let out a shriek before they shot upward. Her heart spiked to rocket speed, and her wide eyes lifted beseechingly to his.

He put his lips softly against her ear. "Don't be so afraid. You're perfectly safe. This stuffy building, as you call it, is state of the art. I'm on a committee that oversees maintenance issues." His deep voice was a comforting rumble.

"You're right," she said. "I'm fine."

"Let's make sure, why don't we?"

When he caught her closer, her breath hitched.

"Oh, my God. You're as cold as ice and shaking. Don't tell me I'm going to have to give up my penthouse view and move to a lower floor."

She was too foolishly pleased that he'd said he'd move just for her, too pleased he was holding her close. She pressed herself against his powerful body and gasped when she found him rock hard and fully aroused.

"See, you make me even crazier than this elevator makes you," he whispered. "I can't help myself where you're concerned. I don't care who you are or what you've done."

His words cut. "But I care what you think. If you don't see me as I really am, how can we ever have a real connection? I'm not the bad person you think I am. I'm not your ex-wife, you know," she murmured.

"Why did you bring her up?"

"Luke told me she married you for your money."

"Leave her out of this."

"Did you love her?"

"I don't want to talk about her."

"Well, FYI—*I'm not her.*"

His jaw tightened, but he didn't argue.

"I'm just a dull working girl."

"A very attractive one."

"You prefer glamorous."

"Maybe we should concentrate on the present," he muttered bitterly. "You have plenty of charm."

His hard arms tightened around her, and he drew her closer—so close she forgot to be afraid, so close she forgot to be logical or sensible. All that mattered was his fierce power and the raw desire she saw in his eyes.

Her hands wound into his silky black hair. In the restaurant, she'd barely been able to think because of his intense gaze and dominating presence. He'd been so nice for the past three days, and then tonight he'd swept her away with the meal and his sexiness.

He bestowed a soft kiss on her forehead. His gentleness and unexpected kindness lessened her doubts.

Maybe he'd loved his wife and had been hurt. Maybe if he moved past that he would be able to see Bree more clearly.

"Hold me," she whispered. "Hold me forever."

Standing on her tiptoes, she pressed her lips

gently to his chin, tempting him to kiss her for real.

"Now who's seducing who?" he teased in a triumphant tone.

"Don't be so impossibly conceited. As soon as we're off this elevator, I'll remember how terrible you've been to me because you're determined to think me a horrible person, and I'll want to avoid you all over again."

"In that case, I'd better seize the advantage while I still have it."

Pushing her back against the wall, his lips found hers. He kissed her hard and long, plunging his tongue into her mouth again and again. Glorious heat rushed through her veins as she kissed him back. Her heart still knocked, but no longer with fear. Reading her response, he lowered his mouth and kissed her nipple through her shirt.

He lifted his head. Dazed, her heart racing, her mouth open, her eyes met the wildness in his gaze. He was the father of her unborn baby. In spite of all the walls she'd tried to erect against him, she still felt connected to him.

What she really wanted was for him to love

their child and maybe someday love her, too. And when he kissed her like this, some idiotic part of her believed that could happen, that he might change some day, that he might see her as she was and be capable of respecting her...of loving her.

When the doors opened, he took her hand and tugged her into his dimly lit hall. He pulled her to his door, which he unlocked. In the entry, he slammed his door and locked it. Then he scooped her into his arms and carried her to her bedroom behind his kitchen, all the while kissing her as if he'd been driven mad by forced abstinence.

"I've been a fool," he whispered, "to deny myself when you make me feel like this. When no other woman, not ever, has come close to affecting me the way you do. The last few days with you have been hell because I've wanted you so much. I don't care how you manipulated my brother."

She wished he'd quit saying that. Will had demanded she marry him—for the baby's sake.

"I...didn't manipulate Will."

"Shh. I don't care."

"But you don't believe me—"

"I don't care."

But she did. Why couldn't Michael wrap his mind around that?

He was the one who had manipulated her and gotten her pregnant. Will had felt so horrible that his brother had abandoned her that he'd insisted she marry him.

Gently Michael laid her on the bed and then followed her down. She opened her eyes and met the heat of his gaze as he smoothed her hair from her fevered brow and kissed her lips, nose and throat.

"I don't believe in happily ever after," he whispered as his mouth moved lower.

"I know." He didn't listen to her or believe her or even *see* her. "Believe me—I get all the bad stuff about you."

"But I'll give you everything else…if only you'll live here and become my mistress."

"No."

"I want you. Never again will you have to worry about money or losing your bistro. I'll take care of you…and Will's baby. No matter what you say, I know those things matter to you."

Money, she thought but with only the faintest irritation. He wanted her, and he still thought she was so low that he could buy her. Their relationship was just another negotiation, a deal to him, terms to be established, services to be rendered for money that would be owed.

She got him, but he didn't get her. Did anything other than money and closing deals really matter to him?

Money wasn't the most important thing to her. Far from it. She was going to have his child. To her, *that* was all-important. Would that even matter to him if he knew? And if it did, what kind of deal would he propose?

She could not be with a man like him on a permanent basis.

But being with him tonight was a different matter. Tonight his passionate ardor had stirred her past caring that he was incapable of giving her what she really wanted for herself and their child—a lifetime of commitment and happiness, tenderness, trust and love.

Deliciously pinned beneath his massive body, knowing he would soon strip her and fill her, felt so pleasurable she didn't want to think about all the negatives. Dimly she remembered her plan to pack and run, to get herself as far away from him as possible. But she was much too weak to follow such a wise course that might protect her heart from a man who didn't seem to have one.

So she smiled up at him and kissed him on the lips.

Tonight she would enjoy him. Tomorrow, and all the dreary tomorrows after that one, would be soon enough to deny herself.

Tonight, she wanted him far too much to walk away.

She seemed so utterly sweet as she lay radiant beneath him.

His wallet lay facedown on her bedside table, the packet of condoms he always carried inside ripped open. They were naked, and he was buried to the hilt in her slick, satin heat. He inhaled her sweet strawberry scent. She was warm, silky, tight—perfect, just as he'd remembered. Better than he'd remembered. Knowing her better had somehow increased his craving for her.

His heart thudded violently. Primal urgency drove him to withdraw and plunge into her again and again, to rush, to finish, to make this an animal conquest instead of a spiritual connection.

Instead, as if she was infinitely precious to him in ways he couldn't begin to understand, he held her close, savoring this first moment of being joined to her.

Relief that had nothing to do with sex flooded him.

He felt whole.

As a child he'd known the insecurity and the degradation of poverty, known too much about the things his mother had done for money.

His mother had loved him, he supposed, but he'd never felt loved. He'd seen other mothers fuss over their kids. They'd come to games, cheered at competitions, met with teachers or worked in the classrooms. Not his mother, and he'd felt the lack of her concern. She hadn't pushed him to succeed either or even believed that he could.

He, however, had believed that if he became wealthy, he'd have power, respect and happiness—he'd have everything he'd craved as a child, including love.

But it hadn't worked out like that. He'd made it big in the financial sector. Somehow his loneliness and sense of alienation had only increased, until finally he'd let down his guard and trusted

Anya. She'd gutted him, making him feel as powerless as he'd felt as a neglected child. He'd vowed never to allow himself to feel that vulnerable again.

Irony of ironies: here he was again, wanting Bree so much he risked everything for her even though he knew she'd used his brother. The increasingly powerful need he felt for her terrified him.

Being with her felt so good, so immensely pleasurable. Nothing had ever come close to the intensity of his feelings for her. He liked sharing the penthouse with her. All day as he worked, he liked knowing she'd be waiting for him when he came home. He'd enjoyed grocery shopping because he'd known she'd revel in the cheeses and crackers and sweets he'd bought her.

He mustn't let himself feel so much, couldn't let himself want so much. Not with Bree, a woman who'd used his beloved brother.

Money and power were the sources of his strength, not this woman. Maybe money couldn't bring the happiness he'd once believed it could, but it bought some awfully nice substitutes. He had to be content with that.

Bree moved in his arms and whispered his name, bringing him back to the present as she begged him in husky tones to kiss her, to take her, to please, please take her.

His mouth found hers, and her instant response made him want her even more. Where would this end?

Something stronger than he was made a mockery of his best intentions not to yield to his feelings for her. In her thrall, his lips ground against hers; his tongue mated with hers. When she clutched him frantically, he lost all control. Her nails bit into his back as she gasped.

In that timeless moment when she melted and clung, he cried out her name. Shattered, he held her close, and all their differences fell away.

His arms tightened around her as she bathed his face with kisses. She was his, and he was hers, so completely that nothing could ever come between them. Never before had he known such pleasure. Despite his doubts, the experience felt so true and honest happiness filled him.

Slowly the moment of shared bliss ebbed. A few minutes later, when she idly stroked his nape, he tensed. As a small child he'd longed for such a simple caress.

He blinked, terrified that she might sense how much such thoughtless affection meant to him.

She couldn't matter this much. Whatever this was, it had to be controlled, managed, put away.

He could not lose himself completely to her. He would not.

Without a word, he slid away from her burning fingertips and arose, knowing grimly that if he didn't, he would make love to her again and again. And every time they came together, she would increase her hold over him until she was everything to him while only his money would matter to her. He didn't want to feel craven, rejected and alone as he had as a child.

Feeling doomed and miserable at the thought of leaving her, and yet knowing it was a matter of survival to do so, he forced himself to climb the stairs to his own bedroom. He would boot up his computer and work tonight. Work would be his salvation. Surely with work he could drive her out of his heart and mind.

It wasn't her fault that he had not felt enough love as a child or that no woman could ever make him feel loved now that he was a man. But he didn't have to put himself under her power. He would lock this thing away, contain it, forget about it, admit nothing to her.

Though earlier this same evening he'd been looking for ways to keep her here, now he wanted her gone—out of his penthouse.

As for the rest of tonight, he couldn't allow himself to see her again before he had himself firmly mastered. It would take every ounce of discipline and willpower he had, but he was determined not to wreck his life a second time.

Bree felt acute heartache when Michael deliberately rolled away from her and got up, cutting their connection.

She wanted another night like their first. She wanted him to take her in his arms again. She wanted him to say he liked her, respected her. If he did, maybe she could trust him enough to confide the truth about her unborn child.

A compulsion to bare her soul, to reach for him, to seize his hand and pull him back, took possession of her. But instead of begging him to stay as she'd done that first night, she lay still and quiet and watched him walk away. Even when she saw him stop in the doorway and turn, his profile was so stern she refused to call out to him.

Then he walked out and closed the door, and she was left to toss restlessly in the dark, telling herself sorrowfully that his departure was really for the best. She should will herself to sleep. But she was too edgy, and she wanted so much more from him. Counting hundreds of imaginary sheep while she knotted and unknotted the corner of the sheet, she lay frozen in misery for at least an hour.

When he didn't come back to bed, she finally arose and pulled on his overlarge robe. Stealthily, she made her way out of her suite, down the hall and across his vast, opulent living area that was bathed in shadow and moonlight. Avoiding his elevator, she tiptoed up two flights of stairs. His bedroom door stood ajar, a stream of light spilling across the dark hall.

He didn't want her; he'd left her. She should go. But what if something was troubling him? Maybe no one had ever been there for him before. Maybe she could help him in some way.

When she pushed the door open, she saw him

hunched over his computer. In the bright glare of the screen his face was haggard and fierce. He was working; he often worked so hard he forgot to eat.

"Michael," she whispered softly as she slid inside the room. "You shouldn't be working at this hour. Is anything wrong?"

He was shirtless, so she saw every muscle in his powerful back swell and harden when he whirled on her. His strong body was as tough and hard as his brilliant business mind. He clenched his fists, as if he felt the need to defend himself from her attack.

But she had no intention of attacking him.

"What are you doing here?" he demanded so harshly he froze her heart.

"I couldn't sleep," she murmured, seeking to soothe him rather than frighten or anger him. "I was too worried…about you."

"Worried? Right." He sounded edgy, dubious, angry.

Was he afraid? Of her? No, that couldn't be. Not when his black eyes were so hard. It was she who felt terrified that he would reject her or be cruel.

"Have I done something wrong?" she asked. "Tonight was wonderful for me. Even better than before. I hoped… I thought that maybe we could start over."

"I'm fine," he ground out. Then as if he couldn't bear the sight of her, he closed his eyes and turned his back on her. "Go back to bed. I have an important meeting tomorrow. I need to go over a few things as you can plainly see."

Hurt swamped her. Swaying a little, her nails dug into the doorframe. She didn't know how she summoned the nerve to hold her ground.

"You can't work all the time, darling, now can you?" she said gently. Before she lost her courage, she crossed the room and slid her arms around him.

He jumped as if her touch and nearness burned him.

"I'm sure your meeting will go better if you get some sleep," she persisted.

"As if I could sleep with you—downstairs."

"I could stay up here and maybe give you a massage."

"No!"

"Yes! You're much too tense. Your muscles are all knotted."

"Because I have work to do!"

Beneath her exploring fingertips his warm, bare skin was smooth as she kneaded the deep tissue of his muscles. When he slowly relaxed and then sighed as if in defeat, she sucked in a breath and laid her lips against his wide chest.

"I can't bear it down there without you, darling. Not when tonight's our last night together."

He hesitated briefly before slamming his laptop closed and folding his arms around her. "I left you because I thought it was best for both of us."

"You won't be sorry. I'm really very good at massages," she said. "I even took a course once... at night school during a short-lived self-improvement kick."

"Bree, oh, my darling," he murmured, the tension flowing out of his deep voice. "Like I said, I came up here with the best of intentions."

"Did you now?"

"You have no idea what you do to me."

"You have the rest of the night to tell me...or better yet, show me. Whichever you prefer, my love."

His mouth claimed hers in a long kiss that was the sweetest he'd ever given her. *He did feel something.* She was almost sure of it.

Maybe there was hope, she thought. Maybe…

For a long moment, as she pondered the possibility, she didn't dare breathe.

Pulling her closer, he opened her robe and stroked her body, knowing just where to touch to arouse her.

"Oh, God, I want you too much to say no to you." Frustrated by the thick fabric, he yanked it off and carried her to his bed where he made love to her again and again, each time as fervently and as passionately as she'd dreamed of him doing.

He did everything he could to please her, and he was everything she had ever wanted or imagined a perfect lover would be.

If only he could be as good for her in other ways, she thought afterward as she lay in the dark beside him. She'd say yes to him, stay with him and tell him about the baby. Maybe their affair would turn into something meaningful.

With an effort she reminded herself that he cared about one thing only—money.

Funny that he should despise her because he thought she was the same.

It was hard to concentrate on packing with him standing over her, his black gaze watching her every movement. He sipped steaming black coffee she'd brewed for him from a porcelain mug.

"I know it's smart for both of us to end it, but I don't want you to go." His tone was that of a command. "I don't want it to be over. You know that."

When she looked up, his eyes were so hot her tummy turned over. The long night of sex had left her tender both physically and emotionally. She couldn't look at him without feeling too much.

As always he was devastatingly handsome in an impeccably tailored three-piece suit he'd put on for his important meeting this morning. He was dazzling. Would their child be equally so?

"I'll miss you, too." Her voice was choked.

Last night in his arms, she'd been so happy, felt so cherished.

She *would* miss him. Too much. More than was sensible. So what else was new? Angrily she threw a blouse toward her duffel bag.

She had to do this.

Had he ever once told her she could matter as a person to him? No. If she thought there was any hope—any hope at all—that he could ever see her for who she was or really care about her, maybe she would have agreed to the abysmal, degrading terms of his affair on the slight possibility she could make him so happy he would change his mind about her over time.

But he was absolutely incapable of being the kind of man she needed in her life, and he could never trust her to be the right woman for him. So why prolong a relationship that wouldn't work?

Because it works in bed, said a sneaky little voice inside her. *Be fair. Not just in bed. Remember how he was last night at dinner? He deliberately took you somewhere special. He was kind when he tended your foot, too, and protective when he slept all night in that awful chair watching over you.*

Remembering everything he'd done to her last night and how she'd reveled in the expertise of his mouth and tongue on all her intimate body parts, she colored.

They'd had last night. Nobody could ever take that away from her.

"Why won't you move in with me permanently?"

"I need my own place where I can be *me* and have *my* friends over."

"You can have whoever the hell you want here."

"Are you kidding? In this stuffy co-op on Fifth Avenue? Your doorman rolls his eyes every time I walk into the building. I value my independence. And you value yours."

"To hell with my independence. I want you."

"For sex."

"I don't deny it."

"That's not enough. If I stayed, I wouldn't respect myself."

"Why the hell not? This is the twenty-first century."

"Because to you, our relationship would just be another business arrangement. Everything is a deal to you. You pay—I continue to sleep over, only in your bed. It's as simple as that."

"No. That's not how it would be." But he spoke sheepishly.

"Isn't it? You don't want a real relationship with

me based on respect and trust, and I don't want to be with a man who doesn't really *like* me."

He changed tack. "But you do admit that you enjoy me…as much as I enjoy you?"

Again she blushed. "That's hardly the point. You think all I've ever wanted from you and your family is money."

"Well, I know you like me in bed, so maybe not *all*."

"See!"

"What do you mean, *see?* Okay, I didn't want to mention this, but since you're forcing the issue, I know that you had my brother set up a million-dollar trust fund for you and your baby. And that you got him to sign it over to you on the day he married you."

"*I* got him to sign it over to me?"

"You heard me! Do you deny you signed documents to claim those monies on your wedding day?"

"Get out! Go to work! Go to your precious meeting! This is what you've been thinking about me all week…and last night when we were making love? A hibernating snake in a frozen hole in the dead of winter has a warmer heart than you do."

"I'd be a fool if I refused to face facts."

"I don't want to sleep with a man who always thinks the worst of me. What can't you understand about that? You'll never change. I'm glad you brought this up because now I can leave here without caring if I ever see you again!"

Tears stung her eyes, but she didn't want to cry. She couldn't give him the satisfaction of knowing how much he was hurting her. Why couldn't he have just asked her about the documents? Why did he always assume the worst?

"Did you or did you not sign them the day you married my brother?" he demanded.

"Yes! Yes! Yes!" Her voice dropped to a whisper. "You've got that part right. I signed them."

When a single tear tracked down her cheek she scrubbed at it furiously with her fist and turned away.

"But it didn't happen like you said, Michael!" she blurted out through strangled sobs. "Or for the reasons you think. I swear it didn't! But did you ask me for the truth? Ever? No!"

"I'm asking now, and you're telling me not to believe what I've seen with my own eyes—which is your damn signature on a dated document. On your wedding day!"

It had all been Will's idea. Not hers. He'd feared his brother wouldn't do the right thing for her or his child.

But would Michael believe that?

"I'm not what you think, but I'm past caring about your opinion of me. I'm through talking to you, through trying to explain myself. It's hopeless to try to change your mind because you *want* to believe the worst. I wish I'd never met you, wish I'd never slept with you. I don't want to ever see you again! Not for as long as I live! I don't want you in my baby's life either—because I want him to grow up with a trusting heart, which is something you'll never have!"

He went white, absolutely white.

"If you change your mind, call me," he said in a voice that was like ice. "Because I want you, no matter who you are, no matter what you've done."

Every time he said that, he carved out a little piece of her.

When he turned and strode out of the room, she lunged at her duffel on the bed and heaved it onto the floor, spilling her clothes everywhere.

Nine

Michael looked so lost, haunted and alone as he stood by his brother's urn. She couldn't take her eyes off him. It was all she could do not to rush to him and put her arms around him.

She was such a wuss. Was it only two days ago that she'd told Michael she never wanted to see him again?

For the past forty-eight hours she'd missed him horribly. The raw agony in his face when his eyes sought hers compelled her for an interminable second or two. He'd loved his brother deeply.

In that long moment when neither could tear their eyes from the other, she shared his all-consuming grief. Maybe that was all they could ever share.

Besides the baby she was too afraid to tell him about.

Whatever faults Michael had, he'd loved Will and was grieving now. She wanted to go to him, to thread her fingers through his, to pull him close and say comforting words in the hope that she could ease that pain.

What if she told him they were going to have a child, that Will had only married her to protect Michael's future child? Would that ease some of his conflict and grief? Or would it add fresh torment since he despised her and believed the baby to be a part of Will?

He was so alone. Maybe Michael had money, but he'd lacked love when he'd needed it most. And the lack had hardened him. Only Will had seen Michael's faults and loved him anyway. Now Michael had to say goodbye to the one person who'd loved him.

When the preacher introduced Michael, he stepped up to the podium and began to speak, his deep voice filling the sanctuary. The words he chose to celebrate his brother's life were so eloquent, they resonated inside her. Hot tears filled her eyes. Her heart ached for him. Soon everybody around her was sniffing and sobbing, too.

Funny that such a heartless man knew exactly what to say to touch so many. If he could speak like that and love that deeply, why couldn't he love her and their child?

When her tears threatened to fall, she brushed them away. Will was dead. Michael was who he was. She couldn't help him or change him. She had to say goodbye to both brothers, keep her secret and move on.

After the service, when the family stood beside the urn receiving mourners, a middle-aged woman with hard gray eyes and a thin, pursed mouth pointed her silver-handled cane at Bree.

"*You!* I've been wanting to have my say," the woman said. "Michael told me that you were pregnant and injured. But here you are—looking fit as a fiddle."

Suddenly Michael, his face grim, materialized beside Bree. Not that he greeted her by word or smile. He was just there, shielding her from the older woman like a protective force field.

When the woman's brows knitted, Michael's hand touched Bree's elbow

"I saw her watching you during the service, so don't think I don't see how it is between you two," the woman said. "She didn't love Will. If either of you think I believe for one minute she had a real marriage with my nephew or that her baby is his…"

Bree reeled.

"Not here, Alice," Michael warned in a voice of steel.

"You can't stop me, Michael. You're as greedy as she is. It wouldn't surprise me to learn you set some sort of trap for Will and used her for bait."

"Don't be absurd," Michael said. "Leave her alone."

"You can't tell me what to do, and I'll sue you again if you try."

His fingers tightened protectively on Bree's elbow. Drawing her closer, he gave Alice a warning look that was so fierce the woman squinted and backed away.

"Thank you," Bree said stiffly as Alice fled down the aisle.

"I told you…the family can be difficult," he murmured. "She was equally cruel to my mother."

Thankfully the next person to approach them was a lovely older woman with silver hair who was dressed in soft grays and blues.

She clasped Bree's hand. "I've wanted to call you and tell you how sorry I am about Will, but I just couldn't work up the strength…until now. I'm Mrs. Ferrar, Tony's mother."

"I'm so sorry for your loss, Mrs. Ferrar. So very sorry," Bree said.

"I know you are. Tony told me how much you and your child meant to Will." Her kind, sympathetic blue eyes shifted to Michael. "He told me how much you meant to Will, too, Mr. North. I know you will take good care of Bree and her precious baby. Will would want that."

Mrs. Ferrar opened her arms, and Bree stepped into them. "There…there… That's right. Give me a big hug. Tony's service will be tomorrow. I sure hope you'll come. I don't know how I'll get through it if people like you, people who knew Tony, aren't with me."

"I will be there," Bree promised. "Again, I'm so sorry."

"I've been cleaning out their apartment, sorting through Tony's things. You two will have to do that for Will. The landlord told me he already has a new tenant, so he's willing to forgive their lease. So, the sooner, the better."

"We'll take care of it, Mrs. Ferrar," Michael said.

We'll...

"I'll miss them both," Mrs. Ferrar said, "and so will you. Some days are going to be hard for you...really, really hard. But when that happens, you think about your precious baby. I have young grandchildren. And they're so full of life, just their pictures on my fridge are enough to cheer me up. I'll do all right."

Despite the sorrowful occasion, Mrs. Ferrar's warmth cheered Bree. In the future, whenever she became sad or confused, she needed to focus on her baby.

"Mr. North, I want a hug from you, too. Such a shame you never got to meet my Tony. I told Will, and more than once, I was sure you'd like him."

"I'm sure of it, too," Michael said, but the new questions in his eyes when he regarded Bree made her swallow hard.

How long would it be before he figured out the truth? The whole truth?

Michael locked his Mercedes, crossed the street and strode to his brother's building. After an endless week of bleak days and nights grieving for Will without seeing or talking to Bree, he couldn't believe she'd actually taken a phone call from him and agreed to meet him at Will's apartment today. He had Bijou to thank for that, he supposed—Bijou, whom he'd bribed with flattery and with dozens of red roses.

Unsure about the reception he'd receive from her daughter, he felt on edge riding up to Will's floor in the tiny elevator.

If the past seven days without Bree had felt like an eternity, what would a lifetime without her be like?

He had it bad. He couldn't sleep, and food, no matter how expensive or how beautifully presented, tasted like cardboard. Even work failed to distract him.

He wanted her. And not just in his bed.

He wanted to talk to her, to look forward to her company at night when he came home. He wanted to make love to her. But he wanted more than all that—so much more. He wanted her companionship and affection, her adoration. She'd adored him that first night—before he'd come clean and ripped her heart open. He wanted her eyes to shine when she looked at him again.

Last week he'd screwed up a major deal because his mind had been on Bree. Since he hadn't pushed ruthlessly enough, he would have to look for new financing for the deal. He needed to go to Shanghai to sort out a mess over there, but he couldn't make himself get on a plane because he didn't want to leave New York with their relationship unresolved.

Why did he feel so lost and alienated with her out of his life?

Because of his illogical need for her, he felt resentment toward her. Had she suffered at all?

Probably not, he thought. Then his heart leaped when he unlocked his brother's door, stepped into the apartment and heard her singing an aria from *Carmen*. She was a little off-key maybe, but not too bad. Hell—off-key or not, the music was charming. She sounded happy.

She was probably thriving without him. And who could blame her?

"Hello!" he yelled, not wanting to follow that train of thought.

She continued to sing. No reply. Either she didn't hear him or she was deliberately ignoring him.

"Hello, damn it!"

The singing stopped, but she didn't call out to him. Annoyed, he stomped into Will's bedroom and found her kneeling over a box of thick wool sweaters.

"What's with the opera? I thought you were into rock music."

Her quick blush made his gut tighten and his body harden.

"Apparently, Mrs. Ferrar took Tony's player and speakers. So I was singing something Luke was humming earlier at the bistro."

"Luke? I thought he finished his assessment of Chez Z. Doesn't he have his own empire to run?"

"I'm sure he does, but he came by because he's so sweet."

Sweet, my ass.

"He took me to dinner at one of his restaurants last night to show me a few more tricks."

Dinner? *Sweet* had nothing to do with it. He was hitting on her.

"Sorry. I know I can't carry a tune. Luke has the most beautiful voice."

Luke, again. Damn. "You sounded okay. Not bad," he said, grumpily, his mind on Luke.

"What can I do to help around here?" Michael muttered.

She refused to look at him. "Just pack everything, I guess."

"Okay. I can do that."

"Maybe you could work in the living room, that way—"

"Right. That way you can avoid me."

"Did I say that?"

"I was rough on you last week, so you think maybe I should apologize."

"Why? You meant what you said. I'm glad I know what you think of me. Now I can move on."

Her cutting words made him feel bleak as hell. But she was right. He didn't trust her. Why should he? Unfortunately, he still wanted her in his life.

He let out a long, frustrated breath and shoved

a hand through his hair. Not knowing what else to do, he grabbed a box off the floor and went into the living room where he began slinging books into it with a fury. Consumed with her, he worked, banging about in the living room for more than an hour. After he finished unloading the bookshelf, he started on the desk and then the computer.

The drawers were slower going because he couldn't pack papers and files without going through them in an effort to figure out if they were important. After an hour, he'd finished two drawers and filled two boxes. Then he opened the bottom drawer and found it stuffed with discs and flash drives that were labeled as photos and videos.

Curious, he loaded a disk that Will had titled *Our First Night Together and Honeymoon* into the computer, because Michael had to prove to himself once and for all that she'd been lying about her relationship.

But the pictures weren't of Will and Bree; they were of Will and Tony.

In the first series of shots, Will and Tony were

holding hands. In the next, they were hugging. Then the pictures got racier.

In each shot, the two of them wore less. Hell, was this some kind of strip session? When they were down to their briefs, Michael decided he'd seen enough and tore the disc from the machine.

Will and Tony?

He stared into space blankly. Why hadn't he seen what had been right before his eyes? Will had always been so sensitive, so sweet and caring. So damned perfect in all the ways Michael wasn't. Michael remembered how Jacob used to beg Will to bring a girl home. *Any girl,* he'd say. Had he suspected?

I will, Dad. I just have to meet the right girl.

But just after Jacob's death, Will had moved here and become nearly impossible to reach.

Had Will been nervous about introducing Michael to Tony? Afraid Michael wouldn't accept their partnership?

But he would have. He did accept it. Realities were realities. People were what they were. He'd loved Will. Period.

The reason Bree hadn't displayed a single photograph of Will in her apartment was because they'd been friends, not lovers.

Just like she'd said.

She'd been telling the truth about that at least.

So why the hell had Will married her?

Michael remembered his brother's glazed eyes in the E.R. and his final words.

"She's a wonderful girl. Not what you think. In a way, what you did to her was all my fault. So, if you'll just promise me…you'll take care of her, that you'll do this one thing for me, we'll be square."

What you did to her…

What had Will meant? What was Michael missing?

When Michael got up and walked into the bedroom again, Bree looked up absently from the growing mountain of packed boxes.

"What? What is it, Michael?"

"Will was gay."

She drew a breath and quickly averted her eyes. "Okay."

"You knew!"

She swallowed.

"So—apparently everybody knew but me…

even Aunt Alice. This puts everything in a new light."

Her face was flushed and her lips trembled.

"Who got you pregnant? Why the hell did he marry you?"

"It's complicated."

Her answer drove him over some edge. "You've said that before. My work is complicated. I bet this is simple. If he was in love with Tony, if he lived here with Tony, if he was never your lover as you claimed all along, how the hell did you manipulate him into marrying you? Who's the father of your baby? Some other guy I don't know about? Tell me his name!"

"Damn you," she lashed out at him. "I was a virgin when I slept with you. You have to know that!"

On some rational level, maybe he did. But women had been tricking men about their virginity for centuries, and he was too angry for logic to work.

She stood up, her eyes aflame, her cheeks dark with rage. "This from you right now...is too much!"

She was angry, angrier than he'd ever seen her.

Fighting for control, she shut her eyes. Not that she calmed down any. When she opened her eyes again they were so bright they shot sparks at him. "I don't want to talk about this with you. Not even now."

"Well, I do. You had some sordid affair and made my brother feel sorry for you—"

"Used him? Had a sordid affair? This is the final straw! I've had it with you! You always think I'm some cheap hustler! You always think everything is my fault! It's *my* fault we got married! It's *my* fault because I'm greedy and manipulative!"

Eyes aflame, she stared at him for a long moment.

"Well, it's not my fault! It's yours!"

"What are you saying?"

"When you slept with me to drive a wedge between me and Will, I *was* a virgin, and *you* got me pregnant!"

He'd gotten her pregnant? Her accusation jolted him like a blow. He reeled backward.

He'd taken every precaution; he always took every precaution.

"I couldn't have gotten you pregnant. That's not

possible." Then why did his chest feel heavy as he stared into her eyes that blazed with outrage and hurt? It was as if her eyes were a fist she'd rammed inside him.

"Apparently it *is* possible because I *am* pregnant. This mess is your fault as much as it is mine! But unlike you, I take part of the blame because I was the simpleminded idiot who slept with you."

"You're claiming I'm the father, and that's *why* Will married you?" Michael's voice was hoarse.

"Yes! I didn't know who to turn to. Like a fool, I cried on his shoulder. He said you were so set against me, it was up to him to do the right thing. He felt someone in the family had to help me get on my feet. He said you'd had a grudge against all women ever since Anya lied about being pregnant and you married her. He said you wouldn't change your mind about me easily. And, oh boy, how right he was! Your brother had a sense of honor—which you don't."

Her words were sinking in, making sense. Horrible sense.

Pregnant. She was pregnant.

"You're sure it's mine?" he rasped.

"Damn you!"

"Sorry," he growled, hanging his head with genuine repentance.

"Look, I've never been with another man. How many times do I have to tell you that? Not that I'm proud of that fact. I wish I'd been with ten other men before you, men who had hearts. Maybe if I'd been the gold-digging slut you thought I was, I would have seen through you. I wish I was pregnant by somebody else!"

He was going to be a father.

Michael felt too shocked to say anything for what felt like an interminably long interval.

She was pregnant with his child and she'd been doing her damnedest to hide that fact from him. And he didn't blame her for that.

He felt sick with regret. What could he say to her now? What could he do? His thoughts were a painful jumble.

He'd gotten a virgin pregnant and had run off to Shanghai to try to forget her. He had a lot to answer for.

"I did my best to protect you—you have to know that. I did everything in my power to prevent this."

"I know. I remember. *Because I was the last person you wanted to have a baby with*. I'm sure there's a lot of collateral damage with every deal you close."

Her voice cut like an ice shard.

"So," she continued, "here we are. You and I are going to have a baby. What now? How are you going to spin it so I'm the evil one? Do you still think I'm trying to manipulate you the way Anya did?"

"No. You're not like her."

"Wow! I can't believe you said that."

What he couldn't believe was that he'd been so blind to the truth where she was concerned. But so many people lied to him, not only in his relationships but in the business world. Too often the men he negotiated with would say or do anything to make a deal.

Bree was not like Anya or the sharks in Shanghai.

The reality hit him hard as he considered how badly he'd behaved toward her.

She was so different from the women he usually dated that he hadn't understood that she might be genuine.

"Were you ever going to tell me about the baby?" he asked softly.

"Maybe…in time."

"You mean in a year or so? Or maybe in twenty years?"

"Maybe."

After the way he'd treated her, he knew he deserved that answer or worse. "Which was it going to be?"

"I don't know. Maybe I wasn't ever going to tell you."

He raked a hand through his hair. His heart was hammering violently.

God, what had he done? Had he thrown away the best thing that had ever happened to him?

"Damn it, Bree."

"You made your feelings for me very, very clear, Michael, on that first night. And on all the nights since."

His gut twisted. Yes, he'd sweet-talked her and made love to her until she'd become radiant every time he looked at her. He'd caressed her so seductively she'd trembled when he barely touched her. Her every nerve had leaped in response to him, but he'd thought she'd been faking.

She hadn't been. While she'd been sincere with him, he'd treated her as deceitfully as Anya had treated him. He was guilty of everything he'd accused Bree of. Afterward he'd told her he hadn't wanted her, that he'd been lying all along and had only pretended he'd cared about her. While she'd been sweet and authentic, he'd been a blind, brutal, rampaging fool. Now, as he remembered the despair in her eyes that night, he knew her virginal pain would haunt him for as long as he lived.

"Everything's different now," he said.

"Not for me, Michael," she said quietly. "You hurt me. You've expressed your poor opinion of me too many times for me not to believe that's how you really feel."

He couldn't blame her. "I know. I'm truly sorry."

"Michael—"

When she looked up at him, distress and confusion showing in her damp eyes, the suffering he'd caused her tore him apart.

"What I did to you that night was wrong. The things I accused you of, even after the accident, were wrong. I see that now. I did something I'd never do in a business deal. Because it involved Will, I rushed into the situation, thinking I had all the facts, but I was clueless. I'm sorry for what I did to you, what I said to you then, and ever since."

She lowered her eyes and bit her lip. Then she lifted her chin. Her eyes were cool, passionless. "I accept your apology. But none of this really matters anymore."

Because he didn't matter to her anymore.

He took a deep breath. "I want to make this right," he said, "but I don't know how."

"It's too late for us."

"We're going to have a baby," he said. "We need to do what's right for our child…maybe get married, maybe—"

"What? Maybe get married? You're willing to marry me because you feel guilty right now? Or because you want control of your precious North heir? Are you out of your mind? You haven't thought this through. You don't want to marry me, and I certainly don't want to marry you. We'd make each other miserable."

"Hear me out. You're going to have my son or daughter."

"Right. Like I said—your precious North heir."

"Listen to me—"

"No! You hear *me* out for a change! I want to marry a man who loves me for me, who wants to conceive a child with me, who thinks well of me, and you're not capable of that. All you're good at is making money."

When he moved toward her, she went white and shrank against the wall to avoid his touch.

"It wouldn't be about your child being my heir."

"I don't believe you, Michael."

"I still want you," he muttered thickly. "I want you so much, and I don't want to hurt you ever again."

"But you would hurt me. Because you can't love me. You can't love anyone. Money is all you really care about because that's what saved you from poverty. I'm sorry for you, but I've accepted the fact that you are how you are…and that no amount of wishful thinking on my part can change you. I won't change my mind. We come from very different worlds and we are very different people."

The undiluted pain in her eyes pierced his

heart. "I can change," he said. "We'll make it work. Somehow. I swear to you."

"I don't think so." She didn't fight him when he lifted her chin and tried to convince her with a kiss. She trembled when his mouth covered hers, but she didn't move into him or pull him close. Her taste intoxicated him even though she simply waited stiffly until he ended the kiss.

"I want you too much to let you go, Bree. The past few days have been hell for me."

"For me, too. But what we feel about each other doesn't really matter. We don't have the same values. You instantly accused me of sleeping around, and I'm not like that. You care only about money and deal-making…we're not right for each other."

"I lost Will. And now I'm losing you. And our child."

"You didn't lose us. You can't lose what you never had. At least, I keep telling myself that. I can't lose you for the same reason—because I never had you."

"Damn it, Bree—"

"Go back to the living room and pack. I don't want to talk to you any longer."

There was a roar in his ears, a fire in his blood

as he caught her roughly to him again. "You're pregnant with my child, and I want to do what's right."

"Then stay out of my life!"

His mouth was hard when it met hers. He was determined to claim every part of her, to make her see that love wasn't necessary when two people belonged together. She was like the air he breathed, the water he drank, the food he ate and the earth he walked on. He couldn't live without such essentials. He didn't love the air or water or food, did he? He just had to have them, or he would cease to exist.

"Kiss me back, damn it." His command was crisp and impatient. "You know you want to."

Her heart pulsed erratically and her skin warmed with fiery need, but she didn't put her arms around him or lift her face to his or give him any indication that she was tempted.

"No—let me go," she whispered raggedly. "Please, just let me go."

The warmth of her breath against his cheek alone was enough to drive him crazy. "Why? You know the sex would be great."

"I told you," she whispered huskily. "I want to

be valued as a person. Not bought. Or kept. This is just another deal to you. I'm the mother of your child. You enjoy me in bed. I'm not quite as bad as you thought. All in all, I'm a better deal than Anya. In order to get control of your heir, you're willing to marry me."

"Damn it, no." He lifted her dark golden hair and pushed it back from her neck. "I do value you. Or…or, damn it, I'll learn to value you."

"You're just saying that to get what you want. But I know what you really feel and think about me. You've always thought I'm greedy and unscrupulous and can be bought. That's simply your viewpoint."

He lowered his lips to the base of her throat where her pulse pounded. "Because before you, that's all I knew."

"Well, that's not who I am, and I don't want to be with a man who lusts after me but can't respect me. Nothing's different except now you know the baby I'm carrying is yours."

"That's a helluva big difference."

When his hand cupped her breast, and he kissed her again, she shuddered. But she didn't kiss him back.

"I can change. I can learn," he said. "I will try to see you as you are. I will."

"It's too late. Because now it's me who doesn't believe you, Michael. How can I believe anything you say? I'm through. Finished. The suspicions you feel toward others are ingrained so deeply into your character, you'll never rid yourself of them."

"I'm the father of your baby."

"If you insist, I'll inform you about anything that has to do with your child."

"I insist."

"Okay. I'll keep you informed. Other than that, we're through." She picked up her purse and slung it over her shoulder. "I can't even pack up Will's apartment with you. I thought I could, but I can't. You'll have to finish on your own. Or use your precious North money to hire movers. Frankly, I don't care how you handle it."

She turned on her heel and walked past him, out of the apartment, leaving him for good.

Feeling hollow at the core, he stared after her, the tomblike silence of Will's apartment closing in around him.

He needed a drink, so he began to ransack the shelves and open the closets.

Where the hell was Tony and Will's liquor cabinet?

Ten

It was amazing what money could buy. And what it couldn't.

Not personal happiness. Not love.

Not the one woman he wanted in his life.

For two months, she'd avoided him.

Michael, who had jet lag from hell, was staying in one of the world's most opulent hotels while on business in Abu Dhabi. Gold glittered from the walls. The drapes and upholstery were decorated in an Arabian theme without restraint. Many floors beneath him, waves lapped gently at the building's foundation and caused a faint and constant hum no matter where one stood in the hotel.

And still he couldn't stop thinking about Bree.

"May I run your bath, sir?" The butler appointed to Michael's lavish hotel suite spoke politely in an upper-class British accent.

Rubbing his temple, Michael switched off the giant plasma-screen TV and went to the floor-to-ceiling windows that overlooked the sparkling blue waters of the Persian Gulf. "No. You can go. I'm expecting an important business call."

The hotel was otherworldly, over-the-top. Michael had a meeting with the sheikh who owned it. He aspired to build another that would be even more ostentatious, more luxurious and more expensive than this one. It was the deal of the decade.

Normally Michael would have been excited to be here, excited to be asked to be part of such an ambitious project.

But he missed Bree.

She'd sounded so cool over the phone when she'd told him they were having a little boy.

A little boy they'd agreed to name Will.

She'd refused to talk about anything other than her doctor's visit. When she'd finished, she'd hung up.

"I'll call you when I have something else to tell you about our child," she'd said right before she'd ended the call.

Michael missed her so much. More than anything. She didn't answer when he phoned her. She didn't reply when he texted. He sent her roses every day, and every day she sent them back to the florist.

Before he'd left for Abu Dhabi, he'd gone to Chez Z to check on her, but she'd made it plain she didn't like seeing him in person. She'd answered his questions in unenthusiastic, monosyllabic tones before she'd asked him to leave.

When he'd told her his agent had found her a two-bedroom, second-floor apartment in her neighborhood in a building that had an elevator, she'd shaken her head. "Leave me alone, Michael. I don't want to discuss anything other than our child."

"But this is about our child. It's about you avoiding stairs until he's safely born. I'll pay for it."

"This is about your money."

"No. It's about the baby. After he's born, I don't

want you carrying him down five flights of stairs. What if you fell?"

"I'll figure something out on my own."

"You're carrying my son. Why won't you let me do this for you?"

"I know what apartments cost in this city," she'd whispered in a shattered tone that had cut him. "A favor like that would give you financial power over me. I don't want to be dependent on you for anything."

"No way will I let you stay in that apartment and risk our baby on those stairs," he'd said. "Why won't you let me help?"

"You know why. Because you use your money to get what you want. Because you think I'm out for anything I can get from you."

"I don't think that anymore!"

"This isn't a deal. I'm not for sale. Neither is our baby. You've used your money to control people for so long, you don't know any other way. Remember how you used to treat Will? Well, I'm determined never to take anything from you again."

"This isn't about money!"

"With you, everything's about money. I can't live that way, or think that way. It's too cold."

He'd once believed that if he became rich enough, he'd have everything he wanted. But he'd been wrong.

Too often his money had put him on the defensive. All he'd been able to see was who wanted what from him. Waiters wanted big tips. Women wanted jewels. Socialites wanted him to give to their causes. He'd been catered to by everybody because they'd all wanted his money. And on some level he'd loved it, because he'd felt strong and powerful and in control.

Michael didn't know what to do to win Bree back. She'd been a virgin and grieving for her brother. Since Michael was her best friend's brother, she'd trusted him and had shyly opened herself to him body and soul. Then he'd deliberately crushed her.

To win her back, he had to become the kind of man she admired. But how?

What if she was right? What if he couldn't change?

Michael, who sat near Chez Z's cash register, looked up from smearing marmalade on a slice of warm, crusty bread and grinned. Bree was storming out of the kitchen toward him. Her cheeks brightened with indignation and that only made her look lovelier in her tight yellow dress and starched white apron that molded to her lush curves.

When he raked his eyes down her shapely body she reddened even more.

"You have to stop this," she said.

"Stop what?" Michael ignored the desperation he heard in her husky voice.

"Coming to Chez Z every single morning you're in town. Constantly embarrassing me like this. Looking at me like that."

His smile broadened. As always, he was so dazzled by her beauty and the immensity of his attraction to her, he felt momentary hope that she might feel a spark of warmth for him if he kept pushing her.

"Embarrassing you? How?" he asked with seeming innocence.

She yanked out a chair and sat down. Leaning across the table so that her staff couldn't hear her, she said, "You know perfectly well how. You send flowers every day."

"I'm the money guy, remember. They look good on the tables. I'm just protecting my investment."

"You drop by every morning on your way to work. You eat breakfast here. You devour me with those black eyes of yours."

"Devour..." He let the word linger as his gaze traveled to her mouth. "Can I help it if you're the most talented cook in Manhattan as well as the most beautiful?"

"Don't you dare compliment me!"

"Sorry." He bit into his crispy hash browns.

"You call so frequently you've got Bijou feeling sorry for you. Everybody who works here is talking about us and taking sides."

"Who's winning?" he asked flirtatiously.

"Since my vote is the only one that counts—me! So stop! You're supposed to be a powerful CEO. Why can't you fly off to Abu Dhabi or Shanghai or at least hole up in your office and run your empire like a good boy?"

"A man has to eat breakfast."

When his gaze touched her as intimately as a caress, her hand darted to her throat. "We have a rule—I call you when I have something to tell you about the baby, otherwise we stay away from each other. Please, just go."

"That's your rule. I'm playing by my own."

"Which is still another reason we can't be together. Look, I need to get back to the kitchen and supervise the prep work."

"I thought maybe you'd like to see the papers for the foundation I'm setting up in Will's name."

Despite her obvious intention to dismiss him, her annoyance gave way to curiosity. "What foundation?"

"It will provide educational opportunities for disadvantaged boys in this city."

"What's in it for you?"

"Would you believe the pleasure of giving back?"

Her eyebrows lifted. "Your PR guy must have told you that a charitable foundation would improve your image. Am I right?"

Teeth gritted, he swore softly. "That's your unwavering opinion of me? You can't imagine that I might empathize with kids who have it as tough or tougher than I did and want to help them? Or that I might want to honor Will?"

"No. This is probably just camouflage. You're

hoping to make yourself look less like the shark you are to your gullible prey."

"I want to take care of you and our baby. You probably don't believe that either."

"Michael, we're having a kid because we both made a huge mistake in judgment. Huge! We have no reason to be together other than the baby."

"That's reason enough for me."

"But not for me! Why can't you just go away and let me run my bistro?"

"Okay, I get it. You think I'm always motivated by greed—even when I try to do good things. We're going to have a baby. I want to take care of you. Why is that bad?"

She just looked at him. "I've told you."

"What if you're wrong?" he demanded. "What if I can change?"

"What if cows could fly over the moon?"

"What if we could get past our mistakes, huge as they are, and become…er…friends?"

"Friends? You and me?" She lifted her chin and stared at him. "Not possible."

"I'll bet our baby would disagree if he had a vote."

"Even for you, that's low."

"There's one more thing." He hesitated. "I found a building in your neighborhood that just happens to have a vacant first-floor apartment that I thought would be perfect for you."

"Please, please don't tell me you've bought it."

"No, but I want you to take a look at it and see what you think. I'm willing to buy the lease on your present apartment and make the owner a very good deal on the one in this building."

"How many times do I have to tell you that you can't buy me?" She pushed her chair back from his table. "You've finished your breakfast, and I've got a full day ahead of me."

"Right," he murmured. "But just so you know, I'm leaving the keys to the apartment with your mother—on the slim chance that she can talk you into looking at it."

"Leave my mother out of this." She whirled and left him.

He watched her until she disappeared. Then he arose and pulled out the envelope containing the photos and information about the building and the necessary keys. Documents in hand, he paid the bill and tracked down Bijou.

"The apartment *is* perfect! I love the garden. I'll try to talk some sense into her," she said after looking at the pictures. She tucked the keys into her purse. "But she's stubborn…especially when it comes to you. This may take a while…and a miracle. I think I'd better go to church tonight and pray. Yes. I think so, yes."

Bree raced ahead of Marcie on the cracked concrete sidewalk that edged the riverbank. She almost passed two joggers, so determined was she to get far enough ahead of Marcie that her friend would be forced to stop nagging Bree about Michael.

The afternoon was cold and sunny, perfect for a walk in the park if only Marcie would change the subject. The humid breeze that gusted off the silvery Hudson River smelled of the sea while gulls laughed and wheeled above them.

"I really think you should reconsider about Michael," Marcie was saying as she caught up to Bree after stooping to hand a dollar to a street musician playing a trumpet.

Bree, who had finally had enough, stopped

abruptly, and a guy on Rollerblades nearly slammed into her.

"Hey!" he cried. "Watch where you're going!"

"I mean, if someone rich like Michael was interested in me and wanted to 'buy me' as you put it," Marcie continued, undeterred, "I'd let him."

"Look, Marcie, I love Riverside Park. I come here to exercise and relax and get away from my problems. Right now Michael is a big problem. So please stop talking about him or go home."

Marcie's brows knitted as she watched an immense white yacht pull up to the 79th Street Boat Basin. "But a foundation? How cool is that? How bad can he be if he gives a fortune away for a cause like that?"

"He told you about that to manipulate you. He's using his money to buy your good opinion. It's a trick."

"Well, if he created that foundation to win you over, I think it's sort of romantic…and sweet."

"Believe me, he is *not* sweet. He's a cunning manipulator who uses his money for insidious, calculating reasons that profit him."

"He thought badly about you not so long ago.

And he was wrong about you, wasn't he? He sees that now."

"Do not compare me to him."

"I'm just saying he was wrong about you, so maybe you could be wrong about him."

Two bikers whizzed past them.

"Marcie, he seduced me just to make Will dislike me. That's bad. He's not to be trusted. Not ever."

"But he's so-o-o cute…and rich. And…and even if he did seduce you for the reasons you say he seems genuinely interested in you now. You should see the way he looks at you. He's got the major hots for you."

Bree's heart constricted. She knew he wanted the baby, and he wanted her in his bed, but she knew as well that he didn't love her. Her mother had married her father because he'd gotten her pregnant, then she'd complained about it so often, Bree had felt guilty for being the baby in question.

"And, God, all those flowers! I wish somebody half as handsome and half as rich would try to seduce me."

"Did he put you on his payroll or something?"

"Hey, I'm not the only one. Everybody else at the bistro thinks you should forgive and forget."

The only reason Michael wanted her was because she was pregnant with his child, and he wanted control over his heir. His attitude hadn't changed until he'd realized Will was gay and had proof that she'd been telling the truth about only being Will's friend.

"You want to know something—sometimes it's very hard to forgive."

A light must have gone out somewhere in the stairwell because the second-floor landing of Bree's steep Victorian staircase was as dark as a cave.

Bree, who was tired and weighted down by two bulging grocery sacks and her purse, grumbled as she readjusted her load before tackling the final, shadowy flight to her apartment. It was only four in the afternoon, but she'd left Chez Z earlier than usual because she'd been too tired to stay. She was looking forward to a cup of tea and a long, hot bath and maybe a nap when her cell phone buzzed inside her purse.

Don't answer it. Not now.

But after it stopped for a short interval it began ringing again. She set her bags on the dark stair above her and began to dig in her purse.

When she saw Michael's name, her heart beat a little faster. He'd been in Asia for the past five days, and so hadn't been by Chez Z to pester her while he ate his breakfast. Was he back? Was he okay?

Even though she knew she shouldn't take his call since she had no news about the baby, she couldn't resist picking up to find out where he was and to make sure he was okay. But just as she touched the phone and his husky voice wrapped around her, something in the bags on the stair shifted. The sack ripped open and shot a barrage of cascading apples and oranges straight at her.

"No!" she cried as she jumped to catch them before they rolled down the stairs.

"What is it?" Michael demanded. "What's wrong?"

Caught off-balance as she stupidly grabbed for an apple, she lurched to one side. Frantically, she reached for the balustrade and missed, falling backward, tumbling along with her fruit back down to the second-floor landing. At least, she had the presence of mind to throw out her hands defensively. Even so, she rammed the wall so hard a white-hot burning sensation shot through her abdomen.

"The baby," she whispered. "Please let him be okay."

For a long time she lay in a crumpled heap, too dazed and winded to move. As the unpleasant burning in her belly subsided, she thought she heard Michael shouting.

"Where are you? Tell me what happened? What's wrong? Bree? Bree! Are you there?"

The phone, she thought. Her phone had to be somewhere nearby. Michael had been talking to her before she'd fallen? Was he back? Oh, how she hoped he was in the city!

Where was her phone?

With a supreme effort, she sat up and discovered her phone blinking madly in a dark corner.

"I'm…on my staircase," she said shakily after she'd managed to inch her way to the phone. "I fell."

"Damn it, Bree. I told you those stairs were dangerous."

"I think I'm okay. I have to be okay."

"Stay where you are," he ordered. "I'm not far. I'm coming over. I'll be there in five minutes—max."

Good. He was nearby. She'd never felt more thankful about anything in her life.

"No hurry.... I'm fine," she whispered. But he couldn't have heard her feeble protests because her phone had dropped his call.

Realizing she was in one of the building's dead spots so there was no use calling him back, she forced herself to her knees. The last thing she wanted was for him to find her on the stairs and panic.

Pushing up to her feet, she stood. For a second or two, she swayed dizzily. When her head cleared, she grabbed the railing and began climbing, grateful that she hadn't sprained an ankle, or worse.

It was slow going, but once she was safely inside her apartment, she collapsed on her couch and willed the cramping in her belly to stop.

She had to be all right. The baby had to be all right.

Four minutes later she heard her buzzer in the

foyer downstairs. Then Michael rang her on her intercom. "It's me."

"Michael!" Unabashed joy filled her as she hit the button and buzzed him inside.

She heard the thunder of his heavy footsteps as he ran up her stairs, taking them two at a time, never slowing even when he neared the top. He ran through the door that she'd left ajar and rushed to her side.

For the first time since their quarrel at Will's apartment, she didn't try to push him away when he pulled her close. She was much too thankful to be wrapped in his powerful arms while he quizzed her about her delicate condition.

He was breathing hard, and his heart was pounding.

He was as scared for her and the baby's safety as she was.

"How far did you fall?" His unsteady tone told her that he'd feared the worst, that he still feared it.

Did that mean he wanted their baby as much as she did? That maybe his interest in her wasn't just about controlling the North heir?

"Not so very far."

"How are you feeling now?"

"I was shaken at first. But I feel better now." Especially now that he was here. "And lucky. I feel very, very lucky." With a deep sigh, she laid her head against his heaving chest and listened to the violent thudding of his heart. "It's going to be okay. Don't worry so much."

"Your doctor's agreed to meet us at the emergency room just to make sure."

"Michael, that really isn't necessary."

"Shh," he whispered. His eyes met hers. "It is for me, so let me take care of you. Just this once...for the baby's sake."

Upon hearing the very real concern in his husky voice, the lump in her throat grew larger.

"I'm glad you're here," she admitted as she pulled him closer. "So glad."

His powerful arms tightened around her. "Well, that's a first."

She was so happy she didn't object, at least not very much, when the team of paramedics he'd summoned arrived, checked her vitals, strapped her to a stretcher and carried her back down the stairs.

Thankfully, her doctor, who beat them to the

hospital, confirmed her opinion that although she'd been shaken up a bit, essentially she was fine. "I would suggest that you climb as few stairs as possible for a while. And as for resuming intimate relations, I advise you two to take a break for a couple of days. After that, just be careful."

"I like your doctor," Michael said after the man left.

"Because he agreed with you about the stair thing."

"No—because he said we can have sex in two days."

She felt her cheeks heat. She glanced around to make sure they were alone. "Michael! We don't have that kind of relationship anymore."

"I miss it. He just reminded me of how much I miss it." He leaned into her and cupped her chin with his fingers. "I want you all the time, and it's been too long. Way too long," he murmured right before he slanted his hard mouth over hers.

"Don't," she whispered, but when he didn't stop, she didn't push against his chest as she should have.

She was thinking about how frantic he'd been

when he'd arrived at her apartment, how capable and truly caring. Maybe he wasn't so bad; maybe he truly was trying to change.

Or maybe her pregnancy had her feeling more vulnerable and, therefore, more forgiving. Whatever the reasons, she was glad he'd come over and so obviously wanted to take care of her.

When his arms wound around her waist, her pulse quickened. Then he pressed her against his muscular length and her hips arched against him.

At her response, he slid his hands over her bottom. "I missed you, missed this."

Desire licked through her like a hot tide. Unbidden came the realization that she still hoped he could care for her. She still hoped that maybe him wanting her in his life because of the baby could be a fresh beginning.

Suddenly all the emotions she'd been fighting exploded, and she rubbed herself against the bulge in his slacks.

"Too bad we have to hold off...for a couple of nights," he whispered grimly.

She pressed herself against him again and then smiled.

"You're killing me. We've got to stop."

His expression was so tender and his eyes were so warm, they melted the ice around her heart.

Eleven

The city sparkled in the night like a million jewels.

Michael lay in his bed counting his blessings for the first time in a while. Thank God he'd been in town two days ago and had been able to get to her apartment so fast.

Two days! For two whole days, ever since her fall, she'd been nice to him. When he'd come into the bistro every morning for breakfast, she'd joined him willingly. She'd even laughed at some of his jokes. When he'd called to check up on her during the day, she sometimes answered her phone.

He was feeling lucky about sex tonight, too.

Her pregnancy was showing—just a little—but that only made her more beautiful to him. Her tummy, which had been a smooth, flat plane when they'd met, was slightly rounded. The bump fascinated him and made him feel protective.

She was carrying his son. He was going to be a father. Maybe after the baby came, he wouldn't feel so alone.

"This doesn't mean anything," she murmured as she lay down on his bed and eased out of her black lacy bra.

"Right." He attempted to suppress his excitement as his eyes feasted on the silky skin and voluptuously soft curves she revealed. "Of course not."

She was still wearing her pants and he his jeans.

They'd eaten Chinese earlier in the evening because he'd wanted Peking duck, and she'd indulged him by accompanying him to a favorite restaurant that wasn't far from his penthouse.

In a corner booth of a glossy black dining room accented with white marble monkeys dangling from the ceiling and golden dragons encircling the walls, she'd eaten jellyfish and oxtails with increasing rapture. He'd feasted on Peking duck presented with scallions, julienned cucumber, delicate crepes and amber-colored hoisin sauce.

Of course they'd shared, nibbling off each other's plates and feeding each other—although she'd been much fonder of his duck than he'd been of her jellyfish. His glass of plum wine had glittered on their table like an enormous jewel. On their walk home they'd stopped at a chocolate shop for plump, chocolate-covered strawberries. Now they lay in his penthouse bedroom lit with silver moonlight.

They'd talked for hours about themselves. He'd told her more than he'd ever told anyone. At one point, when he'd confessed how ashamed he'd felt of the homes he'd lived in with his mother, Bree had placed her hand on his.

"My mother was a little like Anya. She chose her men for what they could give her. I thought all women were like that."

The soft shining light in Bree's eyes had eased the tension caused by the memories and confessions. Normally he never told such stories because they made him feel weak and powerless, but sharing them with Bree had made him feel closer to her, and less alone.

It was a beautiful night. Not that he had the slightest interest in the sweeping panorama of gilded buildings or the immense park beneath them, all of which had been selling points before he'd signed a contract and applied to the board to purchase the apartment.

No, his body's terrible longings had taken him over; it was she alone who compelled him. But unlike the first night they'd been together, his feelings for her now were honest. He liked her as a human being, and he wanted her to like him, too. He knew it would take a while, but he intended to show her he would never again treat her with anything less than the respect she deserved.

Her breasts were fuller than they'd been that first night, their tips dark and tight. He wanted to pull her close, lick her nipples and revel in her fecundity. But he knew better than to rush her. What they had was still too fragile.

"It's just sex," she said.

Not to him, not anymore.

"Whatever you say…as long as you'll keep getting naked for me," he murmured.

She laughed.

Nothing like a good meal to ease her anxieties and turn her on, he thought.

Finding out that she was carrying his child had made him feel far more closely connected to her. She had never slept with another man. She'd chosen him.

Her justifiable fury and their separation combined with his fear for her and the baby after the fall had taught him that she meant even more to him than he'd imagined. Not that he was comfortable with the depth of his feelings for her.

After her fall, with the help of her mother, he'd convinced Bree to move into his penthouse for a few days. So once again, she was installed in his downstairs guest suite behind his kitchen. He was in the process of acquiring the first-floor apartment he'd mentioned to her earlier, but he hadn't told her yet because he didn't want to argue about it.

For the past two evenings they'd spent the early hours after work together, and in an effort to gain her trust he'd deliberately kept things light and friendly. He hadn't touched her.

After meeting her doctor at the E.R., he'd brought Bree straight home and put her to bed.

When she'd said she was ravenously hungry, he'd ordered pizza and served it to her on a tray in her room. Afterward, he'd sat on her bed and they'd talked. He'd been pleased that she'd wanted to know everything he'd done while he'd been away. He'd loved telling her of his adventures and business problems. Then he'd caught up on her activities in New York. He, too, had been thrilled that the bistro was doing better.

He'd stayed in her room for a long time even after she'd shut her eyes and fallen asleep. He'd liked listening to her gentle breathing, liked knowing she was safe in his home…and that their baby was out of danger.

"Kiss me," she whispered now, bringing him back to the present. "I want you to undress me. Then I'll undress you."

A sizzle of heat shot straight through him. With a long sigh, he reached for her and pulled her close.

Coiled around him, with her breasts nestled against his chest, she fitted him perfectly, like the vital piece of a missing puzzle. Holding her, he felt good, safe, on fire. He would feel even better when he was inside her.

With deft expertise they began to undress. Then with a silent moan, she slid her fingers along his nape.

"Oh, how you turn me on," she said.

"You could have fooled me," he said with a smile.

"I'm probably being a fool again, but I can't help myself." Brushing her parted lips along his jawline, she kissed her way down to the base of his throat.

He made a silent, secret vow to be good to her, to believe in her, no matter what. Maybe in time, he would win her.

He threw his head back so that her mouth and tongue could have easier access. She was warm and soft, everything he needed and desired in a woman but hadn't known he had to have.

He'd missed her so much while he'd been away. Every night he'd lain in his lonely hotel bed thinking about her hair, craving her body and that oh-so-intoxicating scent of strawberries.

Now that she was in his arms, the time he'd spent without her in those lavish surroundings seemed drab and empty. If he'd never met her, he would have gone on seeing and being seen with the world's most beautiful women, but feeling restless and empty because he felt no emotional involvement. He would have gone on closing deal after deal all the while longing for something more. He would have had no idea what "more" he wanted, other than more of what left him feeling so empty.

"Kiss me back," she begged.

Their mouths met, open and equally needy. Once he started kissing her, he couldn't seem to stop.

The tips of their tongues flicked against each other and then mated. Heat flooded him, pulsing between his legs. He wanted her, all of her, especially her heart and soul.

For a long time they necked like teenagers, teasing each other mercilessly by remaining partially dressed until their need grew to such a fever pitch they tore each other's clothes off, their bodies contorting so their mouths wouldn't have to part.

When they were both naked, he gently eased her onto her back, spread her legs apart and positioned himself so that his sex touched hers. She gasped in breathless delight at the liberty.

He rubbed himself against her. "I want to be with you like this all the time. When I kiss you, I feel you here. Even on the first kiss, I felt you here." His voice was so raw and intimate she blushed.

"I feel the same way."

He stroked her hair and stared into her shining eyes that finally dared to meet his. He savored the shy warmth in her gaze as well as the heat of her body underneath him. Then slowly, oh-so-slowly, she arched upward, inviting him, and he slid inside her. Holding on to his wide shoulders, she let out a shudder and tugged him closer.

"Why do I want you so much?" she whispered as she began to writhe. "Why?"

"Just accept it like I have."

"So, I'm doomed…just like my mother before me."

"Don't say that," he muttered fiercely, hating that she felt that way. She'd become so important to him.

He withdrew and then pushed deeper. She cried out and pulled him back. Then he lost all control and carried her over the flaming edge.

* * *

Afterward as he lay sated in the moonlit dark with his arms looped around her perspiring body, she turned to him. "You've had a lot of women and I haven't had anyone else. Since there's a lot lacking in my sexual education, there's something I have to know—"

"Don't," he muttered in a low, hoarse tone, feeling awkward. "Don't ask me about other women. They don't matter to me—do you understand?"

She tensed. "I don't mind about them so very much."

He knew better than to believe that, but he said nothing.

"I mean…sometimes I do mind, just not so much at this moment. I'm the odd duck, you see, who never would…maybe because I was too shy or too busy or maybe because my mother was always telling me that the minute I had sex with a guy, he would have all the power."

"What did she mean by that?"

"The reason she married my father was because she was already pregnant with me. She wanted to have this big career, but she felt she had no say in her life after she got pregnant with me."

He tensed, wondering where she was going with this. "Oh."

"You wouldn't believe how guilty she made me feel."

"What they did before you were born isn't your fault."

"Bijou is not a logical person. She said sex can ruin a woman's life if she lets it, that more good women have been brought down by bad men than she could count, that it's women who always pay the price for mistakes in love. And she paid dearly."

"It's not always just the women who pay," he muttered gloomily, thinking of Anya.

"Bijou didn't want me to ruin my life the way she did."

"Then why has she been okay to me?"

"That doesn't make sense. When I told her I'd made this huge mistake and had gotten myself pregnant with your child, she didn't have much to say at first. She's impressed with you, with who you are, with what you've achieved. I don't know. Maybe she just likes it that you're rich."

"Ouch."

"Well, you asked. She must approve of you for some reason."

He smiled, glad that her mother seemed more or less on his side, whatever the reason.

"So, about those other women," she persisted. "Is the sex always this good?"

"No," he muttered fiercely. "How can you ask that?"

"Curiosity." She ran her fingertip down his nose. "You see, I researched you. I saw who you dated. They're all so beautiful. So much more beautiful than I am."

"Bree, baby, you have to understand—they were just going out with me to get things they wanted. Models are into enhancing their image, their brand. I was sort of using them, too. Sex like that, when it's between two people who are out for what they can get, is like…well, it's like a sport or a commodity that you both enjoy but neither of you feel all that deeply about. I was a single man, in need of an escort to parties and feminine companionship. Don't worry about those women because they don't matter at all."

"I don't matter either," she murmured. "Not really. You're only with me because of the baby."

Was she right? Then why did he enjoy doing things with her so much, like eating dinner, talking and laughing? He'd liked her in bed from the first. From the beginning he'd felt connected to her—even when he'd thought she was after the North money, even *then,* he'd liked her.

She was beginning to matter to him so much it scared him.

Instead of reassuring her, he kissed her.

Spiked high heels clicked impatiently on the wooden floor as the Realtor pointed out the many charms of the truly lovely apartment Michael wanted her to move into.

"Original, wide-plank floors!" Lisa Morris gushed. "Can you believe it? Well, what do you think?"

"I don't know."

"You already live in the neighborhood, so you know how wonderful the Upper West Side is. The people in this building are all young, hardworking professionals like yourself. Michael wants you to have the apartment so badly he's willing to meet the seller's first price. Believe me, sweetie, Michael never goes to contract without

negotiating. You have no idea how utterly ruthless he can be."

"Oh, I have an idea." A very good idea. That's
why she still felt wary about their relationship
even though he'd been so nice of late.

"For a lower floor, the apartment is amazingly
sunny." Lisa's voice was as rapid as gunfire. She
walked to a window and impatiently snapped
open the blinds.

If Michael's high-powered Realtor was small in
stature, she made up for it in presence. She was
in her forties, fit and sexy in her own brash way.
She had big orange hair and bright red lipstick.
Nail polish of the same color matched her bright
stilettos and the huge leather designer bag. Her
short black skirt showed off great legs.

"It's modern," she said. "And cheerful. And
totally updated. The garden makes it so special."

If only the woman would stop pressuring her,
maybe Bree could think.

"You wouldn't have to spend a dime. Not that
Michael would be against remodeling it for you—
if that's what you want. He's made it clear he's
willing to do *anything* to please you."

"I already owe him a lot because of an investment his brother made in my business, so I don't want be obligated to him for this, too."

"I'm beginning to see why he's so taken with you. Unlike the women I've seen him with before, you have principles. But trust me, principles will only carry a girl so far. If I were you, I'd snap this place up in a heartbeat. Then I'd snap him up, too. He's a prize catch, sweetie. Nail the deal and the man before they slip through your fingers and you spend the rest of your life regretting it. This is New York. Beautiful women are throwing themselves at him all the time."

"He's just trying to buy me."

"So, let him. He's gorgeous and he can give you the kind of fairy-tale life girls dream of."

"He doesn't care about anything but money."

"So? Sweetie, what do you think drives this city and everybody who lives here? What do you think buys all the goodies…like this apartment with its lovely garden and historic floors? Money. Always has. Trust me, you're lucky if a chance like Michael North comes once in a lifetime."

"Okay, I'll think about it," Bree said.

"You have my card," Lisa said. Her phone rang as she headed for the door. "We'll be in touch." She smiled, lifted her phone to her ear and was gone.

Giving the apartment a final look, Bree couldn't shake the feeling that Michael was trying to buy her by offering what he'd offered every other woman in his life.

Why say no to the apartment when you no longer say no to the flowers he sends, when you're sleeping with him?

Because I don't want to give in to all his demands until I am sure of what I really want. I don't like being pressured.

Michael was nothing if not relentless.

He could take care of her financially. She understood that. But could he love her?

Bree's heart knocked as she followed Michael's beautiful secretary down the marble hall to his office. She felt tense and defensive about her reason for visiting him on such short notice. The girl, a gorgeous brunette who had introduced herself as Eden, had told Bree in pleasant, hushed tones that Michael had canceled an important conference call to make time to see her.

"I'm sorry to interrupt you without giving you

more warning," Bree said to him as soon as Michael opened the door and dismissed Eden. "I understand you postponed an important call."

"It'll wait." He looked deeply into her eyes. "You look upset. Are you okay?"

When she nodded, he pulled her to him and kissed her gently. Then he let her go. "What is it? What's wrong?"

Putting his hand against her waist, he led her to a guest chair and then sat down across from her.

She felt nervous, so she stared at his office. Compared to the glamorous marble lobby of his building and the waiting rooms and secretary's office outside, Michael's office was Spartan. Other than his sunny corner view of the city, no luxuries adorned his personal working space.

His immense, sleekly modern desk was flanked by equally minimalistic tables with monitors. Floor-to-ceiling bookshelves and cabinets were stacked with documents and file folders. Here, there were no photographs, no evidence he had a personal life at all.

"You have a nice view," she said, feeling the need to say something.

"Do I?" he replied, turning to look at it absently. Then he swiveled so that he faced her again. "I prefer this view," he said, his intense gaze causing her to blush. She'd put on a black dress, dangly silver earrings and a red pashmina just to please him. "So—why the visit?"

Feeling a mixture of pride and anxiety, she pulled an envelope out of her purse and pushed it across his desk.

Watching her, he grabbed it, tore it open with his bare hands, pulled out her check and then whistled. "What is this?" he demanded almost angrily.

"I made out a schedule," she said in her most businesslike tone. "I intend to start repaying you on Will's investment in Chez Z."

"That is not necessary."

"You're saying that because I'm pregnant with your child, and you feel obligated to me now."

His black eyes narrowed. "I am obligated."

"I know how everything's a deal to you...." Her cheeks turned red and her voice faltered.

He flushed darkly. "Our relationship is not a deal."

"I'm pregnant, and you feel you have to take care of me. I want you to understand that even though I am pregnant, I can take care of myself. And from now on, I'm going to do so."

"We're sleeping together. Did it occur to you I might want to be generous to you?"

"I don't want our relationship to revolve around money."

"Then why are you here with this check?"

"It's a matter of principle. A time or two, you proposed that if I slept with you, you'd keep Chez Z afloat. Well, I refused that deal then, didn't I? So, I don't want you to think that because we're sleeping together I don't owe you that money."

"Damn it, Bree. You're having my child. Everything's different now."

"I don't want you to think I'm greedy or that I'm only involved with you because of your money. That's not the case."

"I don't think that. The money's a dead issue to me. So, can we not do this?"

"But I don't quite believe you. You've always bought your women, paid them off—"

"You're not like them, okay? How many times do I have to tell you that I was wrong about you before you'll believe me?"

"I…I don't know."

Sometimes she did believe him. Other times she remembered how he'd crushed her.

He must have seen her face fall because he said, "I guess I deserve that. I know I hurt you badly."

"Let's just say the way you made me feel is burned into me like a brand. I'm having a hard time letting it go."

He cursed softly. "I want to make that up to you. I don't want to hurt you like that ever again. As you know, I had a rough start and got knocked around a lot as a kid, so I'm not always an easy guy—and that's when I'm not deliberately being a jerk. Not that my history is an excuse, but I was prejudiced against your sex after Anya. Now, though…everything's different. I only hope that someday I'll be able to prove to you I've changed my attitude."

"For now—just take the money," she whispered. "It's important to me…in ways I can't explain. I'm going to start repaying you in two-week intervals."

"Okay. Whatever you want. However you want." His cynical tone was low and biting.

When she stood up, he led her to the door.

"One more thing," he said. "Since we're discussing finances maybe now would be a good time to inform you that I signed a contract on that building in your neighborhood."

"Oh, no. I wish you hadn't."

"I know, more proof you're nothing but a financial obligation to me, but hey, why don't you look at this a different way? My purchasing the building gives you choices. You can continue to stay with me at the penthouse. I told you last night how much I look forward to coming home to you. Or if you need more independence you can move into the apartment and be on your own."

"I would not be on my own, if you own the apartment."

"Then you can pay rent."

"I have a lease where I am."

"I'm sure I could work out a deal with your landlord. I don't want to force you to be with me. I just want you and the baby to be safe."

"Okay," she said. "I'll think about it."

"So—do we have any more finances to discuss?"

She shook her head.

"Good." His gaze warmed as he took her hand and drew her to him. Realizing that he wanted her to kiss him goodbye in spite of their disagreement, she softened, too.

Standing on her tiptoes, she closed her eyes and slid her arms around his neck. Against all logic, her resistance melted when his lips claimed hers. Why did she always feel that something was very right in her world when he held her like this?

"See you tonight?" he whispered, sweeping the back of his hand across her cheek.

She nodded. "I'll cook. What are you in the mood for?"

"Not food." His hot glance and quick grin made her knees go weak.

"We were discussing supper," she whispered primly.

"We were?" He arched his dark brows.

She nodded.

"How about steak and potatoes?"

"Okay, then," she said, her eyes aglow as she envisioned juicy slabs of beef topped with mushroom sauce, baked potatoes oozing with crunchy bits of bacon, chives and sour cream. She would buy a deep red wine for him, a burgundy maybe, and crisp garden-grown greens to make a salad for herself.

"Followed by you for dessert," he whispered with a sexy smile right before he kissed her again.

Twelve

Four weeks had passed, and in that time Michael had grown relaxed in his relationship with Bree. She'd allowed him to help her get out of her old lease and move into the apartment he'd bought for her. She'd agreed to pay him the same rent she'd paid her previous landlord.

Tonight, Michael felt heavy and sated after an hour or so of deeply satisfying sex that had followed the lamb dinner she'd cooked for him. Funny how the more times he had her, the more his need for her grew.

Utterly content, he pulled her closer.

The doors to her garden were open. City sounds and moonlight crept over the walls and filled her bedroom. He was glad she'd relented about the apartment. Before she could change her mind, he'd sent a team of movers and packers to her old place.

Maybe it was time he pushed on a much more important issue.

"I want to marry you. I want you in my life forever," he said, speaking softly as his hand caressed her arm. "We've had a month together. I think we work."

He felt her tense, but she stayed where she was.

"We've been over this," she said tightly.

"Not lately."

"You only want to marry me because of the baby—*your heir.*"

Damn it, he thought. Ever since her fall, he'd spent as much time as he could with her because he cared about her. Why couldn't she see that?

He'd taken her to the theater, to movies and out shopping. He'd joined her on her afternoon walks in Riverside Park. They'd picnicked in Central Park, enjoyed dozens of fabulous dinners in New York's top restaurants. Then there were the countless rounds of mutually satisfying sex.

They got along. More than got along. He looked

forward to every moment he had with her. They enjoyed friendship as well as sex. Weren't those things they could build on?

"As soon as I found out you were carrying my child I wanted to take care of you. I asked you to marry me then, remember?"

"Because you felt obligated."

"You said no, and because you felt that way, I've worked hard to develop a relationship with you."

"Because you just see this as the best solution, the best deal. Or you feel you *have* to do this, maybe for the baby—"

"What if I said that maybe I do feel obligated because of the baby, but I want *you* in my life, and that maybe I do...love you."

Hissing in a breath, she pushed away from him, plumped her pillows and sat up straighter. "Well, I wouldn't believe you, Michael." She crossed her arms over her breasts. "So don't do this."

"Why the hell not?"

"Because loving me has never been part of your agenda. You'll say or promise anything to close this deal."

"I admire you. I like hanging out with you. I

can't keep my hands off you. I miss you when we're not together. I miss you so much it consumes me. If what I feel isn't love, it'll do until love comes along."

"Marriage demands a total commitment. For me, it demands love. Even then, there's a fifty percent divorce rate."

"Love is just a four-letter word for a complex emotion that means different things to different people."

"Look, Michael, Will told me you would say anything to get what you want. Look at this apartment. Look at the way you've been sending flowers to the bistro for months. You got my mother and everybody who works for me to badger me until I agreed to move in here. They're all on your side. You've totally won them over."

"So, I've been vetted. Maybe you should take that as a sign we belong together."

"No, I take that as a sign you'll do anything to close the deal. I can't believe that even you would stoop so low as to try to trick me into letting myself believe you could love me. Do you think I'm such an illogical romantic that I'll do what you want if you just toss out the word *love?*"

"You think that my reasons for proposing to you have to do solely with a pragmatic concern for gaining more control over my heir?"

"I didn't at first. In the beginning I was starry-eyed about you. But the way you treated me that first night and right after Will died burned away my romantic illusions. I can't help it if I see you plainly now. I don't dislike you, Michael. Far from it. You have to know I'm crazy stupid about you in bed. And you're fun to hang out with. But this is an affair. Nothing more. An affair I think I'm stupid to engage in because I'm not sophisticated enough to keep my emotions guarded all the time."

"Guarded?"

"Yes. Guarded. I can't let myself care too much again. You have affairs all the time with women like Natalia."

"What I have with you isn't like that."

"I may be naive, but I know that an affair between people like us, who have different values about life, will end. I don't want ours to end now…so let's not discuss this. And let's not talk about marriage, either. Let's just enjoy each other while we can. Later, we'll part, and when we do, we'll work out a way to raise our son, okay?"

"Not okay!" He threw off his sheet, stood up, scooped his clothes off the floor and began to throw them on.

"Oh, so now you're mad at me? This is so unfair, Michael. You're the one who seduced me and got us into this mess. No matter what you say, I know the only reason you'd ever want to marry me is because I'm pregnant with your heir!"

"Well, I don't deny I've been a damned fool when I stupidly thought you were using my brother. If I was prejudiced then it was because I couldn't see who you were. But now you're the one who can't see who I am. For the past month I've tried to show you that I'll be good to you. Maybe I deserve this. I thought we were happy together."

"It has been fun," she agreed.

"It's been way more than fun. But if you don't want this to go any further, then I won't push myself on you any longer. If you think this relationship is all about closing a deal, well, the deal's off."

"Michael, stop this. You've got to see that we

could never have a real marriage. My mother married my father because she was pregnant with me and she was miserable. The only thing you and I have in common is the baby. You do international deals. I'm the owner of a bistro. I'd hold you back."

"The hell you would."

"You'd resent me just like she resented him. Why don't we just enjoy our affair until its natural conclusion…and then we'll figure out a way to raise our baby together?"

He felt raw and sick to the core at that prospect—devastated. Bitter pride made him mask the deep wound she'd inflicted.

"If that's the way you really feel, maybe you're right." His voice was cool. "Maybe you are better off without me. I've given it my best shot. I'm through."

"Michael!"

He tore his key to her apartment off his key ring and flung it on her bedside table. "Consider our affair concluded. No deal."

His heart wasn't in what he was saying as he shoved his shirt into his slacks and picked up his cell phone. Why couldn't she see who he was now? Why couldn't she accept that he truly wanted to be with her? That he could come to love her? That he didn't want this half-assed deal she was proposing?

As he strode out of her bedroom blind to any emotion other than his own hurt, he willed her to come after him.

But she didn't see who he was, didn't feel the pain that was choking off his breath and she didn't follow him. When he left the building, he prayed that she would call him on his cell and agree that what he felt for her was enough. Love grew day by day, like a flower, didn't it, if it was real? Hell—what did he know about love?

When his cell phone buzzed, his heart raced. Thinking it was Bree, he grabbed for it, but it was Natalia, of all people, so he declined the call.

As he looked up from the sidewalk, he saw Bree standing in her window wrapped in a tangled bedsheet.

She was as pale as a ghost. Did he only imagine the shimmer of brightness on her cheeks? His heart constricted. Had he made her cry?

He wouldn't let himself care. She'd rejected him.

When she let go of the curtain, and it fell back

into place, he tore his gaze from her window and hurried down the sidewalk.

When Natalia called him again a few minutes later, he picked up. Why the hell shouldn't he?

Bree stared up at her bedroom ceiling. Feeling lost and uncertain, she'd been staring at it for hours.

With shocking, devastating suddenness their affair was over.

Bree had known she'd be hurt when he left her, but the pain that pulsed in the center of her being cut like a blade. It was as if all hope for happiness was draining out of her like blood seeping from a fatal wound.

Hours later, when the sun turned the rooftops in her neighborhood bloodred, she got up, dressed and walked out of her apartment, feeling heavy from her long, sleepless night.

Hoping to clear her head, she made her way toward the park. She wanted to be around noisy cars on their way to offices and schools, around people rushing to catch buses or subway trains. Near the park, she bought herself a bagel and coffee from a street vendor and kept walking.

Michael had said he cared about her, that he knew he craved her, missed her.... And because she'd been a fool to believe him before, she'd refused to let herself believe him now.

But what if he'd been telling the truth? She remembered how tenderly he'd treated her when she'd fallen on her stairs. He'd said he'd been happy with her this past month. She'd certainly been happy with him.

What if he *had* come to care for her? What if he *could* love her? What if this relationship wasn't just a deal to him?

What if she was wrong? What if he'd been telling her the truth? What if he didn't feel trapped into marrying her? What if he really was beginning to fall in love with her, and instead of giving him a chance, she'd driven him away? What if she'd hurt him with her rejection exactly as he'd hurt her?

Oh, God. Thinking herself a naive fool, she pulled her phone out of her pocket and called him.

"What do you want?" he said, his tone so harsh he terrified her. "I'm on another line."

"Michael..."

The line went dead.

She wanted to hold on to his voice, but he was already gone.

She caught a slow, agonized breath. Had he deliberately hung up on her?

Motion on the street seemed to stop as she clasped the phone against the violent pounding of her heart. The horns and sirens around her grew silent. The hawker's voice died away. The pedestrians passing her seemed to walk in slow motion. All she could feel was the pain in her heart.

She felt like screaming, like crying out, but of course she did not. Instead, she stumbled back to her apartment where she waited in her living room for over an hour for him to call her back. When he didn't, she set her phone on an end table and picked up her purse.

She took the key to his penthouse off her own key ring. She dug an envelope out of her desk, addressed it and put his key inside. Leaving the package on the table, she walked outside to water the ivy that climbed her garden wall.

While she watched water from her hose rain

down on the bricks, she tried to imagine how she would live the rest of her life without him.

"Aren't you sleeping?" Bijou demanded.

"I'm fine," Bree said, annoyed by her mother's constant hovering of late.

"Why the dark glasses then? Afraid I'll see the shadows under your eyes? Why aren't you sleeping?"

Bree yanked off the offending glasses and tossed them into her purse. "I am sleeping!" she lied. "Why wouldn't I be sleeping?"

She hated it when her mother poked her long nose where it didn't belong and kept poking it— which had been happening way too often lately.

"No more flowers?" Bijou persisted.

It was now day two after Michael had walked out on her, day two since he'd stopped sending flowers.

Bijou lifted a vase from a table in the main dining room and removed two withered roses. "Did you have a quarrel? Or is this more serious?"

Bree wasn't ready to talk about Michael. "Why don't you go check on the prep work? Or maybe sweep outside?"

"Why hasn't he been coming by for breakfast anymore? I miss him."

"Bijou! Please!"

"Should I maybe call him, yes? And tell him we miss him, very much, yes?"

"No!"

"So—you did quarrel. Then you foolish, sad girl, you must call him and make up!"

She'd tried, hadn't she? And he hadn't called her back.

"You don't know anything." When Bree's eyes began to sting she went to her purse, grabbed her sunglasses and slammed them back on her face. "Please. Don't ask me about him right now."

"You two are so romantic," Marcie whispered from a table in the back. "Such passion. Such fire."

Not anymore.

Her life felt empty, colorless.

Feeling hollow despair, Bree shut her eyes.

"You're just as unhappy as he is," Luke said as he set his fork down. "I came by because I thought that would be the case."

"It's just an off night," Bree countered defensively as she stood over his table.

"Yes. Everything about this place is off...*you,* the service, the pastries, the soup, even the omelets, which were always perfect, but especially you. Since I know what you're capable of and what your staff is capable of, you can't fool me. A month ago, you were doing so well. This place was fun. Hot."

Since Michael had walked out two weeks ago, she'd had to force herself to go through the motions of living. She knew she hadn't been concentrating at work.

"I'm sorry if your dining experience has been such a disappointment."

"Bull! What's going on between you and Michael?"

"Nothing."

"Funny, he said the same thing when I went to check on him."

"You've seen him?" She tried to keep her face blank but her heart had begun to race.

"Yesterday. Did you know that he's all but withdrawn from the world?"

"We haven't been in contact lately, so—no."

"Really? Well, he's taken the week off—hell, he never takes a week off—he's a ruthless work-aholic for God's sake! Right now he's just sitting around his penthouse reading. Or watching his cleaning lady do her tasks. *Watching his cleaning lady!* He's not shaving or showering. She took me aside when I was leaving. She told me she's worried sick about him. He won't answer the phone—especially if it's Eden, his secretary, calling about work.

"I asked him about you. I said if you love her, for God's sake, man, tell her. He looked up at me with eyes that were as dark and dead as death. You know what he said?"

She shook her head.

"He said, 'I tried, Luke. But I guess I don't know what love is. Or at least she doesn't think I do. Or I'm not the man she wants. Do you really think I didn't try?'"

Bree sank into the chair across from Luke. Had Michael really said all that?

"Thank you for caring about him. And thank you for coming by to check on me. It was sweet, really. Thank you."

"So—are you going to call him?"

"I don't know. He broke up with me."

"Call him. He loves you, woman."

Did he? Did she dare believe that she was really more than an obligation or another deal he had to close?

She thought about the way he'd grown up… without ever getting enough love. Maybe he did love her. Maybe love was such a new experience for him, he wasn't sure what it was or how to express it.

She remembered how sweet he'd been after her fall, how committed and determined he'd been to have her in his life ever since.

He could have any woman he wanted, and he'd chosen her.

Maybe he *did* love her. Maybe she'd been wrong.

Whether he truly cared or not, she was worried about him. Should she go to him? Check on him? After all, he was the father of her child. They would have to talk at some point. Why not now?

But what if he wouldn't let her in?

Her key. Since she'd procrastinated as usual, the envelope with his key was still in her purse, waiting to be mailed.

* * *

When the intercom buzzed for the fifth time, Michael got to his feet, swaying slightly. How many shots of scotch had he had? Who cared? He'd lost count.

On unsteady feet he crossed the room that was littered with newspapers and business magazines and answered his intercom.

"It's me, Natalia."

Surrounded by media, she looked gorgeous on his video screen.

"Go the hell away," he said.

"Carlo, I told you about Carlo, he jilted me. He thinks he's this big important producer. But nobody jilts Natalia publicly and gets away with it. I was so wrong about you, wrong to blame you for anything. Carlo—he is the real bastard."

"Well, I'm sorry about Carlo, but I can't talk right now."

"Can I please come up?"

"I said this is a bad time, Natalia. Look, you're a beautiful girl. Sooner or later your luck with men will change."

Platitudes, he thought. Who was he to give advice to the lovelorn when he was in a lot worse shape than Natalia?

He cut the connection and poured himself another scotch. Then he slumped onto his couch again and tortured himself with more memories of Bree—Bree with her cute baby bump climbing on top of him, Bree taking him into her mouth, Bree kissing him everywhere with those little flicks of her tongue that drove him wild.

What the hell was he doing, dreaming of a woman who didn't want him? Luke was right. He couldn't go on like this.

Michael had brought this on himself. She saw him as deal-maker, not as a husband. He'd offered her all he had to give and she'd rejected him.

She was the mother of his child, and he had to establish a workable, familial, brotherly relationship with her so they could raise that child together. That was all that was left, their bond as parents.

With Michael's key clutched tightly in one hand and her purse in the other, Bree walked up to his building just as Natalia emerged with a smile meant to dazzle the paparazzi lying in wait for her.

"Yes, I'm dating Michael North again," she said to a reporter when he thrust a microphone to her lips. "He invited me here." When flashes blazed, she laughed triumphantly and raced for her limo.

An inner voice cried inside Bree. *See how easily he replaced you with someone more beautiful. You were just an obligation, a deal he wanted to close. Go home. Forget him.*

On the walk through the park from her place to his, visions of married life had flooded her mind. She'd imagined Michael beside her when the baby came, Michael beside her at their son's first birthday, Michael beside her at the holidays and dining at home with friends. And all the while that she'd been imagining a shared life with him, he'd been entertaining Natalia.

She flung the key into the bottom of her purse. Lacking the strength to walk home, she went to the curb and asked the doorman to hail a taxi for her.

Somewhere a bolt turned in a lock. Michael blinked, annoyed at the sound. Dimly he grew aware that someone was outside his front door fumbling with a key. Who the hell could it be?

Natalia? Hadn't he sent her away? Despite the liquor that fogged his brain he was almost sure he had sent her away. He hadn't given her a key, had he?

When his door gave way, he shot to a sitting position in time to see a woman glide gracefully inside.

"Natalia?"

The great room was filled with gloom and long shadows and his vision was blurry from drink, so he couldn't make out her features. Still, something didn't seem right. Natalia was several inches taller, wasn't she?

"Not Natalia. It's me, Michael," said the soft feminine voice he'd dreamed of for days.

A pulse in his gut beat savagely.

"Bree?"

"Yes."

When she turned on the lights, he blinked at the glare and sat up straighter, pushing back his tangled hair. When was the last time he'd showered or shaved? Why did he give a damn? She'd turned him out, hadn't she? She saw him as nothing more than a crass deal-maker.

"Why are you here?" he demanded coldly.

She shut the door and moved cautiously around the newspapers that littered his floor. She moved as if she was approaching a dangerous wild animal.

Aware suddenly that he wore the same T-shirt and pair of jeans he'd put on yesterday, the same ones he'd slept in, he flushed. His eyes burned as he studied her, and his head ached.

Damn it. He didn't want her pity or her tenderness.

"Tell me what you want and go," he growled fiercely.

"Luke came to the bistro and told me…you weren't well."

"The two of you should mind your own damn business. As you can see, there's nothing wrong with me. I'm fine. Having the time of my life! Go home."

She picked up his empty scotch bottle. "Looks like we've got one dead soldier. Why don't I make you some coffee?"

"Because I don't want coffee," he snarled.

"Well, maybe I do. Why don't you freshen up so you can play host while I putter around in the kitchen?"

"What gives you the right to barge into my house and boss me around? We broke up—remember?"

"I'll be happy to tell you why I'm here after you take a shower and make yourself presentable. You really don't look very civilized, darling." Again her voice was maddeningly light and cheery as she disappeared into his kitchen.

He considered going after her, but when he took a step in pursuit, he stumbled. Feeling unsure, he thought better of following her.

One glance in his bathroom mirror had him shuddering in disgust. Who was that man with the narrowed, bloodshot eyes and the greasy, tangled hair?

Ashamed at how low he'd sunk, he stripped and stepped into an icy shower.

The cold water was hellish, but it revived him. Five minutes later, when he returned to the great room, he'd shaved, brushed his teeth and slicked back his damp hair.

She smiled. "You look like a new man."

Except for his headache, he felt a lot better. Not that he was about to admit it.

"Why the hell are you here? If you've come because you pity me, so help me…"

"I don't pity you. I love you. I've missed you. Picnics in the park. Dinners out. And the passionate things you did to me in bed. I think I'm okay with you thinking maybe you love me."

He looked down at her, unable to comprehend her words.

"What?"

"Drink your coffee," she whispered as she handed him a steaming cup.

His hand shook slightly, but he took a long sip and then another. It was strong and black, just what he needed.

"What are you saying?" he demanded.

"Luke came to see me."

"Oh."

"I was worried about you, so I came over. Then I was so scared when I saw Natalia downstairs in your lobby. She was all but holding a press conference and telling everybody you two were back together."

"We're not back together," he said.

"I know. The doorman told me you hadn't let her up. If he hadn't told me that while he was helping me hail a cab, I would have lost my courage and gone home."

"We haven't been together since I called it off months ago. Her new boyfriend broke up with her and she has such low self-esteem she goes crazy when that happens. She can't stand to feel abandoned or rejected, so she came over here. But I was in no shape to deal with her."

"It's a very difficult feeling…abandonment," Bree whispered.

"Yes, it is," he said.

"That's how I felt that first night when you told me you'd lied and didn't care about me."

"I'm so sorry." He sucked in a breath. Without Bree these past few weeks, he'd felt as if he was a dead man. Now that she was here, he felt alive again. "I missed you," he whispered. "I missed you so much."

She sat down and put her arms around him. "I love you, too. I love you enough for both of us. I'm going to hope that what you feel for me will grow…as you said it would."

"Bree. I do love you. Now. And forever. If I

didn't know it before, I know it now. You don't know what I've been through…without you. I couldn't work or think. I was utterly worthless without you. I want you and our baby…more than anything."

He set his coffee cup down as she circled his neck with her arms. Her hands moved gently through his hair, which was still damp from his shower.

"You really love me?" she said.

Their eyes met. "Yes, these past few days I haven't been able to forgive myself for how I treated you. You don't know how I despised myself. You were so sweet and wonderful that first night. And I never gave you a chance. I tried to crush you. And I nearly did. I couldn't blame you for not trusting me."

"We both must forget about that night."

"Never. It's the night I first began to love you…I just didn't know it or couldn't admit it. Forgive me…please."

"I do. Oh, I do."

He took her face between his hands, his thumbs lightly brushing her lips. "I thought I'd lost you, and I didn't know how I'd live without you."

"I felt the same way. Isn't it wonderful we don't have to live without each other?"

It was too wonderful for words.

He kissed her long and hard. He pulled her closer and kissed her again and again, drinking of her deeply, tasting her, reveling in her nearness, her sweetness, until they were both breathless. "I will never get enough of you."

"I love you," she said again.

"Yesterday, I dreaded all the tomorrows of my life," he murmured. "Now I'm looking forward to them. You, dear, sweet Bree, have freed me from myself, from Anya, from all the dark emotions that hardened me."

"If I've helped you even a little I'm very glad."

"You've given me such happiness, a whole new life."

His lips claimed hers, and he didn't let her go for a very long time.

Epilogue

Never had Bree felt so content, so proud of herself, nor so filled with love and affection as she did right now. Lying in her hospital bed she watched Michael pace proudly, his voice soft as he tried to soothe their darling, newborn son.

Michael was such a good husband. Every morning she woke up loving him a little more, and she knew he felt the same. Not only had he stayed with her during labor and stood beside her during the delivery, he'd gone with her to every doctor's visit and to every childbirth class she'd taken.

Baby Will's eyes and hair were as black as ebony. The instant the nurses had laid him in her arms she'd fallen in love. She'd uncurled his fingers and he'd wrapped them around hers and hung on. Maybe she loved him so much because he was a tiny replica of his handsome dad.

Michael walked over to the bed and leaned down to show her their son was sleeping. As she lifted back the blue blanket to stare at her son's wrinkled, red face, a great rush of tenderness swept her.

She was the luckiest woman in the world.

"Michael," she whispered. "Isn't he wonderful?"

"He is, and so are you. I love you," he said in a low tone that shook her to the depths of her soul. "I love you more than anything in the world."

His words shook her because she was sure, so very sure, he meant them. Deep down, he'd always been a family man. Even though he'd been wrong about her in the beginning, love of his younger brother and his fierce desire to protect him was what had brought them together. He'd wanted his brother to experience the kind of love he'd never had himself, but had craved.

She was so glad she saw who he really was now—a man who had found the love he must have been looking for his whole life.

He was a fighter. He would always be there for her; he would always love and protect her.

Yes, she was the luckiest woman in the world to have this man and be loved by him.

* * * * *

MILLS & BOON®

Why shop at millsandboon.co.uk?

Each year, thousands of romance readers find their perfect read at millsandboon.co.uk. That's because we're passionate about bringing you the very best romantic fiction. Here are some of the advantages of shopping at www.millsandboon.co.uk:

* **Get new books first**—you'll be able to buy your favourite books one month before they hit the shops

* **Get exclusive discounts**—you'll also be able to buy our specially created monthly collections, with up to 50% off the RRP

* **Find your favourite authors**—latest news, interviews and new releases for all your favourite authors and series on our website, plus ideas for what to try next

* **Join in**—once you've bought your favourite books, don't forget to register with us to rate, review and join in the discussions

Visit **www.millsandboon.co.uk**
for all this and more today!